A
Journey
of
Sunsets

A Journey of Sunsets

An Adventurous Story of Beauty, Transformation & Discovery

Nashyelli Elena Hernandez

From the Coffee Shop Series

To Benjamin Liam & Nadia Renée:
Of all my life's adventures, being your mom has been
the greatest one.

Journal Entries

Thoughts from the Author

There is a common sentiment often attributed to spiritual and philosophical traditions that says, "We [humans] have explored the depths of the ocean and the vastness of space, but the greatest unexplored territory lies within ourselves."

For years, I filled journals with ambitious to-do lists, eagerly checking off each adventure as I completed it. I craved experience - the perfect photograph, the next adrenaline rush, each accomplishment carefully displayed for my social media friends to like. I was hungry to show those around me that I was an explorer, risk-taker, and overachiever. And so, I found myself jumping out of planes, scuba diving to the bottom of the ocean and becoming even a billboard model. I set off on many trips in the name of adventure, exploration, and the next high. Yet beneath it all, I was traveling around the world escaping from myself, my lack of confidence, and low self-esteem.

It is astonishing to now realize I could travel alone to the other side of the globe, venturing to the furthest corners of the earth; yet I was scared to travel solo to the unexplored territory of my own soul. This inner hesitation left me vulnerable with emotional holes, easily manipulated by the claws of materialism and the pressuring voices of society dictating my identity and, often, my path. The truth is, I believed it all, simply because I had no idea what lay inside.

In 2011, after reaching an emotional rock bottom, I found my way to the transformative practices of yoga and meditation. These ancient disciplines invited me on a profound journey inward, where I unexpectedly discovered an inner sanctuary – a sacred space of peace, contentment, and the undeniable truth of my being. Suddenly, I realized I was never "holey"; the idea of incompleteness was merely a lie created by my own mind.

This newfound awareness also revealed a beautiful truth: that the journey within has no final destination. We are all endless travelers and forever pilgrims of life. Each day, regardless of our age, level of intelligence, or background, offers us a fresh opportunity to learn something new about ourselves and the boundless universe within.

As I was having all these realizations, the idea of writing a book came to me in 2015, sitting at a Café in Rishikesh, India. While I had no idea exactly where to start, I knew that if the idea had chosen me as a vessel, I had to rise to the occasion.

For almost a decade, I set off on a writing journey where somedays I would write a sentence, others multiple pages. It wasn't until 2024 that I knew I had to press on to finish what I had started and now here we are - you are holding in your hands many writing years of my life. Know that as I was working on this book, I was embarking on my own journey to the soul.

A Journey of Sunsets is a book blending beauty, transformation, and discovery with components of fiction and non-fiction throughout, with each page capturing experiences around the world, real life lessons, and thousands of thoughts.

This book tells a story of beauty – the kind of simple beauty that you find in the melting colors of a sunset, the sweet smile of a child, or in the comforting aromas of brewing coffee on a rainy morning. This will show you that beauty is not related to perfection as I saw beauty buried in the poorest villages of India, further reinforcing the idea that for as long as you are looking for beauty, you will always find it.

This is a story of transformation - you will find references all throughout the book from a sun moving across the sky starting in a quiet pre-dawn at the edge of awakening until dipping below the western horizon at the close of day. You will also find that this story transforms grieving into empowerment. Sometimes, we must die to learn how to live – die to old habits, negative thinking patterns, and the heavy baggage that no longer serves us. In many aspects of the story, the mom and Brenée transform into one as they both walk a similar path.

This is a story of discovery - as you travel within, you discover the truth of who you are. This book is an invitation to the realization that the pearl you were looking for in the depths of the ocean or the star you hoped to find in the vastness of the sky has been in you all along.

The moment you are willing to travel within, you'll discover there is no longer a need to search without.

My wish, dear reader, is that once you decide to embark on your own journey of sunsets, the journey within, you do not get distracted by the noise of the world, your fears, and judgements. Keep walking. Do not lose sight, for the most meaningful landscapes of yourself are just coming up.

Happy travels...

*The Journey One
Must Take
Is the Journey
within…*

~Nashyelli

August 18th:
Under the Southwest Sky

The morning air was warm, holding just a hint of the Southwest Texas desert heat. The horizon remained a serene canvas at 5:15 A.M. and there were no signs of a pre-dawn light in the eastern sky. The city was peacefully asleep, and the streets in the residential area were relatively quiet at this early hour.

The faint chirping of crickets and the occasional call of a desert bird in the distance could be heard in the dark. The crisp breeze with a scent of desert flora could be enjoyed, like creosote bushes and mesquite trees, adding a distinctive fragrance in the mornings. In the stillness of this peaceful scenery, the silhouette of the Franklin Mountains was visible in the dim light, creating a picturesque backdrop to the city. And then there were the stars; the stars that under a cover of darkness with muted purples and blues made the sky a celestial masterpiece.

Under this heavenly canopy, it was easy for the early risers walking the dogs or enjoying a morning run to feel humbled by the immerse vastness of the sky above. That early morning, however, as the clock ticked closer to sunrise, the stars led a path of unexpected tracks.

A female runner of medium build and athletic shape took the first running step to cross a major intersection where she had the green pedestrian light.

Glancing both ways, she could see the lights from a car far off.

It looks like the city is slowly starting to wake up, she thought. *I hope my family is doing the same.* With no reflective vest on and in the dimly lit street, she continued her steps into the crosswalk.

The driver, weary from a long graveyard shift, sat slouched behind the wheel, struggling to stay awake. His eyelids drooped as the hum of the engine, coupled with the rhythmic sound of his blinker, lulled him into a near-daze. The dashboard lights blurred his vision, and the driver blinked slowly.

Suddenly, at the turn of the intersection, from the corner of his eye, the driver saw a shadowy figure dart out of nowhere in a split second. The driver's heart leaped, adrenaline surged through his veins as the sleepy haze vanished at the violent slam of his brakes. His tires screeched against the asphalt trying to avoid hitting the person he hadn't seen. The car jerked fiercely, and everything in the cabin shifted forward with force.

Despite his efforts, the car struck the dark silhouette, causing her body to hit the hood landing hard on her head fifteen feet away from the initial impact. The driver's once drooping eyes were wide open, fully alert, breathing heavily, and gripped by the sudden shock of fear. With no time to spare, the driver opened his door and rushed towards the body.

In a moment of total stillness, the female runner took a last inhalation and transcending beyond the moment, she exhaled her last.

At a house three miles away from the scene, the alarm went off abruptly waking up Brenée.

"Ugh, stop it!" Brenée groaned as she hit the off button with her hand emerging from underneath the covers. *I don't feel like going to class this Monday morning,* thought the young lady after briefly going over her class schedule in her head. Stumbling out of bed, Brenée glanced at her reflection in the bathroom mirror, noticing her long, wild, and tangled hair. "Would you look at that? Today is hoodie day," the 21-year-old woman with a slightly, slouched posture, and inward-rounded shoulders said to herself.

Slipping her dark hoodie over her head, Brenée pulled the ties tight on both sides, her face disappearing into the shadows of the hood. Hidden. Small. This was no surprise to her parents, who despite numerous efforts, often noticed Brenée conveyed a sense of hesitation, self-consciousness, and a desire to hide from the world.

As she could hear her family already in motion, Brenée's dad was downstairs beginning to make the first pot of coffee for the day. The rich soothing aroma of brewing coffee wafted in the air, filling the house with comfort as the morning began.

"There she is!" Her dad greeted Brenée with a kiss on her forehead. "I see you're ready to take over the world!" he continued with a sarcastic tone over Brenée's unobstructed look.

"Hi, dad. Not today. I'm not in the mood for it." Brenée replied in her usual passive voice while giving dad a soft kiss on his cheek.

"Alright, alright! What's wrong? Is everything ok?" he asked wanting to hear more from Brenée.

"Nothing really. Just woke up with this strange feeling in my gut for some reason, dad. It's probably the fact that it is Monday."

"I can understand that. I'm about to make some scrambled eggs. Do you want some?" he asked changing the topic.

"Yeah, that's fine," she replied, "Hey," she continued with a slight furrow in her eyebrows. "Where's mom?" she asked out of curiosity.

"She mentioned last night that she was going for a morning run. I'm sure she's on her way back," he said. "Come on, get ready so we can all eat breakfast together before you go to class," her dad said, and she agreed with a head nod.

Continuing their morning routine as usual, it wasn't until breakfast was ready and the first cups of coffee had been enjoyed that she thought it was strange her mom was not back yet. With a growing sense of worry, Brenée approached her dad again.

"Mmm, dad? Isn't it odd that mom is not back yet," Brenée said with a nervous voice.

"You know how spontaneous your mom is. She probably bumped into someone she knows and decided to grab a coffee with them. I called her, but she left her phone in the bedroom. Come on. Let's eat before you leave. Food is getting cold," her dad replied.

"Uhmm, you are right. On my way to class though, I will check her usual running route."

"OK, pretty girl," he replied as they both sat down at the table to eat. "I'm not sure what you have going on after school," he continued, "but if you can, stop at the west coffee shop to make sure business is running as usual. Lisa, one of our Baristas, is out and they will be short-handed today. Your mom and I will be busy in a meeting with the SBA applying for a business loan to expand the east shop."

"SBA? What's that?" Brenée asked as she kept eating and looking down on her plate.

"Shouldn't you know that by now, Brenée? It's the Small Business Administration," her dad answered with a certain frustration in his voice.

"I don't pay attention to that, dad." Brenée said making it sound as if she was stating the obvious.

"Ohh, I know. You seem to live in your own world. Anyway, please try to help us today."

"Ok, dad. Gotta go now."

Getting in her car, Brenée started her drive to class with her mom still in mind. While paying attention to her mother's usual running route, Brenée approached a main intersection three miles down the road before the highway when she noticed an area cordoned off and the lane closed.

Her heart stuttered as she saw the remains of what appeared to be an accident scene.

The area had been cleared of emergency vehicles for the most part, but something deep inside told Brenée to pull over and ask what had happened. Parking on a side street and rushing out of her car, Brenée reached for a police officer who was making his last reports.

"Excuse me, officer," the young woman said from the distance with a slight reluctance to engage. "I'm sorry to interrupt you, but can you tell me what happened?"

"There was a pedestrian accident," the officer said as he turned his body to face her. Brenée's breath caught in her throat and with a shaky voice she continued asking.

"Mmm…was it a woman? What was her name?" The police officer, confused about Brenée's multiple questions, replied while walking closer toward her.

"There was no form of identification or a cellphone on her. Why are you asking?"

"Well," Brenée answered trying to avoid eye contact, "My mom went for a morning run. When we woke up, she was not home. My dad and I don't know where she's at and she regularly runs this route."

She noticed the officer's attention sharpening, focusing on her explanation.

"The body was already transported out of the scene. I could take you to the medical examiner's office so you can see if the victim was your mother. But please stay calm; it may just as likely be someone else."

Brenée could only nod with hope as fear enveloped her heart.

"Okay, follow me there."

Brenée got back in her car and immediately called her dad with the speaker on, taking a moment before following the police car.

"Dad," Brenée said with a knot in her throat. Her father instantly could tell something was going on as Brenée's usual passive voice turned expressive, heavy with emotion.

"What happened, Brenée?" he asked.

"Is mom back yet?" Brenée asked one last time, holding on to the faintest glimmer of hope in her heart.

"No, she's not. What's going on?" he asked again. Brenée could hear the anxiety in his voice ripple through the phone line. She shivered, clearing her throat and finally managing to get a few choppy words out.

"Dad, there was an accident at the corner of Vista Del Sol and Yarbrough. Someone died. It was a female, and she had no ID on her!" Brenée burst into tears with sobs racking her body as the fear became too much to bear.

"Calm down, Brenée. Where are you?" her dad asked.

"I'm about to drive off to find out if it is mom's body," Brenée replied.

"Brenée, please wait for me. Don't go alone! And stay calm, there is a chance it is not her," her dad answered with a composed voice that gave her a sliver of faith. "I'm getting in my car right now. I'll be there in five minutes."

"Okay, dad. I'll wait," Brenée replied trying to regain some control over her breath.

Brenée and her dad, who arrived in no time, followed the police officer to the morgue. Like a record on repeat, she kept focused telling herself "Mom is alive, mom is alive" for the whole drive.

When they arrived at the morgue, the police spoke to a few people then took Brenée and her father down the hall into a cool room. As they crossed the threshold of the doorway, their eyes were led to a body lying on a cold steel table draped with a white sheet. It almost appeared as if a single beam of light descending from the sky was shining on the body. In a detached tone coming from the forensic specialist, Brenée and her dad were instructed to get closer to identify the victim.

Exposing the face by partially removing the white cloth, her breath vanished for a fraction of a second after realizing it was her - her beloved mother lying dead on the table. A weep turned into a shout and Brenée started yelling uncontrollably, hugging the motionless body.

"No, Mom! No way! Why, mom?" She felt her father's arms wrapped around her, holding her tight as if to keep them both from breaking. Tears streamed down her face and her body trembled from the recent discovery.

On that hot desert day in the summer month, Elena's body had been identified under the Southwest Sky.

August 30th:
Uncovering the Unknowns

Gone at 44 years of age with so many goals left behind, the sad news of Elena's passing quickly reached the ears of those who knew her both as a friend and business owner. After all, Elena had dedicated much of her life to turning the art of a good cup of coffee into a thriving business.

By her relatives, Elena was also known as a devoted mother and loving partner, always unconditionally loyal to her family even if her passions kept her perpetually busy. Some might have said she was a little too driven at times, living life in the same way that she enjoyed her coffee, filled to the brim.

The cremation arrangements took place without delay. That was because Elena had left clear instructions that she didn't want a formal funeral. The idea of solemnness, sadness and regrets had no place in her plans. If anything, she wanted a life celebration for the final day.

A late August afternoon, her family organized a gathering at home where those who loved her came to share fond stories in front of her ashes. Many people attended, more than she probably ever expected; all expressing how Elena had touched their lives. Although there were tears, there was also a sense of joy and celebration for her life.

For Brenée, however, there was nothing to celebrate.

During the days following the funeral, she began sleeping for long hours, keeping an inconsistent schedule at school and spending most of the day in her room. Instead of trying to move through her sorrows, her loneliness took a sharp regression leading to severe depression.

It was a cool crisp fall morning two months after Elena's passing, when her father decided to try again to connect with Brenée.

"Brenée? Pretty girl, can you open the door? I know you are hurting," her dad spoke from behind the closed wooden door. "I am hurting too. But your mom wouldn't want to see you this way."

The bedroom door clicked as the lock turned, followed by a faint creak with the handle being pushed down. "I know, dad," Brenée appeared behind the door with her eyes red and swollen as a sign she had been crying for hours. "It's just hard to accept that she's not here anymore." She went back to bed to bury herself under the covers. "Mom was the only one who understood my world and now…now, she's gone. I don't know how to stop hurting. I miss her every day."

"I do too, but we can't just be in a box trapped in our sadness. I am sure your mom would not want to see you this way," her dad said as he stood next to her bed. "It would be good for you to step out of this room and find something to keep your mind busy. Maybe stop by to help me out at the shop today, or maybe you could…uh," he paused to gather ideas, "Maybe you could go through some boxes your mom left in the office room. Once you've sorted through them, we can decide what to keep and what to donate."

"I'll see what I can do, dad. Okay?" Brenée replied in a tone that suggested she wanted to be left alone.

"Okay, I'm off to the shops now," her dad said with sadness taking off to work.

Later that afternoon, Brenée managed to drag herself out of bed. Still wearing her pajamas and with her hair tied back in a messy ponytail, she headed to the family office downstairs.

Gently swinging the French doors open, she found the stack of medium-sized boxes her dad had mentioned by the right corner of the room. Brenée sat down cross legged on a rug covering the floors and lined up the boxes in front of the door.

She leaned slightly forward as she took a deep breath and gently blew a soft puff of air across the surface of the boxes. A small cloud of dust rose and swirled in the air, catching light from a nearby window. She watched the dust particles dance, revealing the boxes had been sitting in that room for some time.

Opening the first box, she found a collection of things without any apparent value that her mom had gathered from the places she visited. One in particular attracted Brenée's attention, a collection of dry leaves and small rocks with the name of the places and dates of visit written on them in black ink. A small smooth rock of light grey color read "Ireland, 2015." Brenée grabbed a copper-colored rock next, "China, 2013," then a dry maple leaf, "Canada, 2022." Brenée took the different rocks and leaves one by one reading the words written on them. And just like that, Brenée realized these little items were valuable treasures after all.

Putting the first box aside, she proceeded to open the next one. Inside the second box, Brenée found some books, a couple of magazines, and journals. Fanning quickly through the pages, Brenée didn't feel the need to keep any of the books and magazines.

When she got to the journals, however, something caught her attention. She noticed there were three journals with her mom's handwriting and the first one reading "Brenée" all across the cover. *For me?* she thought as her head tilted to the side, showing a mix of intrigue and confusion. She held it with some hesitation and cautiously opened the cover of the first journal as though it might reveal a deep secret.

My Dear Brenée,

When you read these journals, my time in this world will have passed. I hope my words don't bring you grief over my departure but rather inspire joy in my life well lived.

Truth be told, I had fun!

My wish is to live for many years to come and witness you grow into a remarkable woman, but if I don't, my dear, I would love for you to live a life filled with creativity, adventure, and exploration. Always remember, life is a path with unpredictable twists and turns and when you get to the end of the line, we take absolutely nothing material with us. In fact, we will only take the memories we created.

Driven by my adventurous spirit, I do not wish for my cremated ashes to stay at home, let alone stay trapped in an urn. Instead, I'm requesting for my ashes to be released in meaningful places of special significance to me during my lifetime.

I have left a list of places where you will stay and a fund for you to cover the expenses to be incurred by my request.

You are to travel solo first to the city of Delhi next February that comes after my passing.

Perhaps that is coming in a few days or maybe you need to wait a few months. Either way, it is time to prepare. Upon your arrival in India, I will guide you where to go next.

While it may be tempting to read ahead and uncover the full travel plans, I ask that you follow my instructions and reveal each step as it unfolds.

Brenée paused in a state of great perplexity. *Wait a minute…India? How is this possible? Did mom discuss her wishes with dad? Is that why he asked me to look through these boxes?* Brenée thought looking for answers. She took a quick peek through the rest of the box, but there was nothing else except the other two journals.

In a flashback, Brenée recalled her mom's journaling habit and the way she meticulously wrote plans for everything that mattered to her.

Does it mean mom had a plan even for a sudden end? She wondered, baffled and puzzled. She thought about calling her dad, but instead, she resumed reading, burning with curiosity.

Her mom's instructions concluded:

I understand if fulfilling these wishes becomes emotionally challenging, but it is very important to carry out these plans. It gives me great comfort to think that my final wishes will be honored, and I will be resting freely in places that hold treasured significance to me.

Love you to the sun and back,

~Mom

As she concluded reading the page, it appeared her mom's directions were detailed in the three journals, which involved three different trips to three different countries.

Love filled Brenée's heart, and a profound sense of closeness coursed through her body in a way that words alone couldn't describe. Seeing the flow of her mom's unique loops, curves and strokes in her handwriting stirred a mix of deep, tender emotions. She felt a sense of warmth and nostalgia in the tangible reminder of her mother's presence, bridging any distance between them.

Brenée closed the journal with both hands in a soft, gentle movement, tucking away her sadness and feeling a sudden spark of joy.

That night after her dad came home from work, the young woman approached him.

"Dad, I'm sorry I didn't go to work today to give you a hand. But I did go through mom's boxes like you asked me to."

"It's okay, Brenée. Are the boxes ready for me to take for donation?" her dad asked.

"Well, no dad. Not exactly. While I was going through the boxes, I found some items mom collected during her travels and among them, three journals mom wrote to me. Did you know about the journals, dad? Did you know about mom's plans?" she asked.

"Plans? Journals? What are you talking about, Brenée?" her dad asked as he looked at his daughter with his full attention.

"Mom left in writing that she does not want her ashes to stay at home. She didn't even want them inside an urn like they are right now. Mom wants her ashes to be spread around the world, and she wants me to do it," she explained.

"She never discussed that with me," her dad replied with a puzzled expression. "You? Alone?"

"Yes, I mean…I get my mom's final wishes, but I don't understand why me. I feel like she's asking me to dive into the deep end when I don't even know how to float!" Brenée said with wide, anxious eyes.

"Well, we both knew your mom. She was a force! This sounds very much like her all-or-nothing mindset," the dad said with a smirk in his face perhaps recalling countless times he found himself in the same situation. "That reminds me of a story your mom once told," he continued. "A tiny seed sat quietly in the soil, surrounded by towering trees. The seed envied their height and strength, but it felt too insignificant to grow. Over time, the sun warmed the earth, and the rain nurtured the ground. Slowly, the seed began to sprout. Its roots grew deeper, and its tiny stem reached higher. At first, it trembled in the breeze, unsure if it could stand tall. But as the days passed, it realized the same sun, rain and soil that nurtured the tall trees were within its reach too. Then, with each passing season, it grew stronger, until one day, it stood as tall and proud as the forest itself.

You are like that seed, pretty girl, gradually growing and getting stronger. Trust your mom and more importantly, trust yourself. I know you can do this."

Listening to her dad ignited a small spur of curiosity about her capabilities. "You really think so, dad?"

"Of course! When have I lied to you? You know I always give you my honest opinion," her dad said as he reached out for her hair, softly tucking it behind her ear.

"Yes, dad. You always do. Mom wants me to leave next February. At this point, I have four months to mentally prepare for it," she said pointing to the calendar on the wall.

"Let's sit and make some plans. Oh wait…. show me your mom's journals first. I would like to see them."

Seated in the kitchen, Brenée's dad kept listening to her recount of her discoveries, uncovering - one by one - the unknowns in the box.

December 25th:
Summer Holiday in the Winter Cold

It was the turn of the winter in the Southwest desert and Brenée's departure was only a couple of months away. Perhaps not enough time to fully prepare for her time away, but Brenée and her dad trusted the path was going to be revealed by her mom step by step. Since the discovery of the journals, Brenée started helping her dad at the coffee shops, slowly letting go of her depression.

A few days before Christmas, the whole family gathered at Brenée's house to spend their first holidays without Elena. Family members from both sides traveled from out of town to see Brenée and her father, providing much needed support. Brenée was especially thankful to see Grandma Emily, Grandpa James, and Abuela (grandma) Manuela (affectionately called "Abue Nela") before her travels began.

"Christmas does feel different without her around," Brenée's dad said as they were gathered around the dinner table.

"It sure does, son," Grandma Emily replied.

"How do you feel about your trip, Brenée?" her grandfather James quickly asked to shift the conversation away from the heavy sadness they all could feel.

"I'm nervous, grandpa, to tell you the truth. I'll be traveling for months alone and even as I say that right now, I feel the heavy weight of the task pressing on me. There are times I wake up in the middle of the night sleepless in disbelief asking myself, what was she thinking? Why did she think I was the ideal person to do this? Did she forget I am not like her? I am not daring like she was! But the conflict is…" Brenée paused for a moment stopping her complaints, "That these are mom's final wishes and I feel like I have to do this."

"You must trust your mom, Brenée. She knew exactly what she was doing when she chose you for this task," Abue Nela stated with pride in her voice. "Your mom was not always like you remember her. She was in fact quite shy in her younger years - much like you. She learned to ride a bike and swim as an adult because as a child, she was often afraid. I think it wasn't until she was in her late twenties that things drastically started to change. She became an adventurous spirit, a daring soul," Abue Nela recalled. "And from then on, there was no turning back."

"I remember the stories she would tell me about her travels," she continued, "like that time she went to Argentina and started conversations with some random anti-government street artists in the dark basement of a building they squatted in thousands of miles away from home." Abue Nela paused to emphasize, "picture this…your mom drinking yerba mate with…*who knows what kind of people…* in God knows where, listening to their stories and stance against the Argentinean government. Who in the right mind does that?!" Abue Nela said making a hand gesture of disbelief.

"She did that?" Brenée interrupted with eyes wide open. "That is…dangerous!" she said in awe.

"Oh, I know!" Abue Nela replied. "I believe she was making up for lost time and those were the kind of experiences she was willing to have."

"So, was mom not born adventurous, Abue Nela?" All eyes turned to the old lady as they waited for an answer.

"Ahh! That's a good question, sweetheart. Well… your mom was the living example that being adventurous is both, born and made, a blend of ingredients provided by nature and nurture. Take for example a coffee bean – during harvesting, the best quality beans are chosen based on their natural qualities such as color, firmness and size. But then, it's not until they go through the roasting process that the real magic starts to happen. Beans endure pressure, heat, and time to start releasing their aromas becoming sweeter and more complex. Flavors begin to develop and the longer the roast, the richer and more robust they become. Isn't this then born and made, Brenée? Isn't it then the art of blending both that makes it possible for you to enjoy a good cup of coffee?" asked Abue Nela as she sipped on her black coffee.

"Your abuela is right, pretty girl," her dad focused on Brenée again as he reached for her shoulders. "Your mom knew your natural skills; she saw that beneath your shyness lay a quiet strength. We all here see it, Brenée," her dad pointed everyone around the dinner table as they agreed.

"We do," Grandma Emily added. "If it helps, think of it as joining the study abroad program. I think that will lighten up the heaviness you feel, don't you agree? And speaking of school, what will happen with that? Isn't this your senior year?" she asked.

"Well, dad and I talked about it and I am pausing college for now, grandma. That is the only way I can meet mom's timeline and leave to India next February." Brenée exhaled a calming sigh, allowing her words to sink in.

"Pausing college is a big decision, but I trust you are doing what you feel is best," Grandpa James said. "Let us know if there's anything we can do to help."

At the Christmas Eve dinner, Brenée looked around the table, her heart aching with the absence of her mother. Yet, at that same moment, Brenée felt an overwhelming wave of affection from the rest of the family like never before.

With a sad heart, but wrapped in warm love, they made of Christmas a summer holiday in the winter cold. At the dinner table, any traces of disbelief were shattered. Brenée was going to India - in a couple of months, she really was.

February 12th:
A Dive into the Sky

After two months of anxious anticipation, the countdown to February 12th ended. The morning was quiet at 4 A.M. and Brenée's flight was four hours away; however, it was almost impossible for her to continue sleeping.

Mom, the day has come. Guide me. She thought as she sat by the edge of the bed and opened the first journal to read the words of her dear mom.

Hello, my Sunshine.

Embrace the adventure ahead!

Today you are answering the call to begin the journey to India. Yes, it will be a long, tiresome, and perhaps even frightening trip, but allow curiosity to guide you, savor each moment, and welcome the unexpected.

This very moment brings back the memory of when you were only a little girl. On rainy nights, you would get scared of the sound of thunder, running into my arms for peace and protection. What I never told you, my dear, was that, from time to time, I would get scared of life too and it was only in your arms that I would find my ground and direction.

Brenée, my girl, you are not alone. If this feels like a rainy night, know I remain by your side when the thunder strikes. Here, you are in my arms.

 Once you get to the airport, come back and see me again.

Love you to the sun and back,

~Mom

Brenée closed the journal with comfort in her heart. And even though she didn't get more information, she remembered the words from Abue Nela to trust her mom.

To calm her nerves down, she decided to go through her packing checklist again before closing her backpack. *Zzzzzzrrrrrr* – The zipper made a gentle, repetitive, and rhythmic sound as Brenée pulled the slider from left to right. *Click, click* – the two black buckles on the front of her bag announced the mission was about to begin.

Brenée carried her backpack with her as she walked out to the kitchen where her dad was already brewing a fresh cup of coffee, a familiar aroma she would miss.

Dressed in a comfortable outfit, she wore a well-worn black jacket, a soft scarf loosely draped around her neck, and a pair of old sneakers for the long trip ahead.

"Morning dad. You are up early too," Brenée said with a slight strain in her voice attempting to mask her nervousness.

"I couldn't sleep," Her dad said while giving her a soft kiss on her forehead.

"Same here, Dad."

"Listen Brenée," he paused carefully choosing what to say next, "I know you can do this, but…but if it becomes too much, come back home please. Don't think you will disappoint us. Your wellbeing is more important, and I am sure your mom would agree. Remember what we talked about and please, make sure you stay in touch, so I know you're okay."

"Of course, daddy," Brenée replied while reaching for his arms much like that feeling of her mom around her on a rainy night. "Thank you for reassuring me I won't disappoint you and mom." In this silent exchange of connection, where no more words were necessary, Brenée and her dad hugged for a long time almost trying to make the moment last forever with no rush to pull away.

When their hug had to end, the bittersweet departure for the airport commenced. With the passing of each mile, Brenée watched the house that cradled the memories with her mom slip away.

The silence in the car was thick, punctuated only by the low hum of the engine and the occasional click of the signal on the turn ahead.

Once at the airport, her father parked the car so he could walk her inside, further stretching out their goodbye as if trying to extract every second from the clock.

"Did you remember to pack your mom?" her dad asked, nudging her playfully to take away from the heaviness of the moment.

"Well…yeah, dad!" Brenée replied, bumping him back with a cheeky grin.

As they strode through the airport, Brenée tried her best to portray a figure that exuded a sense of composure. In the inside though, a mix of emotions rippled through the air around her.

Despite their efforts to delay the inevitable, they both knew time couldn't be stopped and Brenée needed to head up to the security line at the bustling airport.

Stepping onto the escalator, Brenée literally felt the ground beneath her feet shift, carrying her upward without turning back. Brenée looked down, letting go of the moving rail to waive at her dad with sweaty palms.

"I'm going to miss you, daddy," she yelled in the distance waiving her hand.

"I'm going to miss you too, pretty girl," he said with love, worry, and pride.

As the moving steps carried her higher and higher, her dad and her comfort zone slowly slipped away. Finding her footing on solid ground at the top gave her enough stability to get in line. With passport in hand, she waited to go through security. To keep her anxiety at bay, she counted the three boarding passes, briefly scanning departure information. But her heart raced even more as she read the third boarding pass, showing Delhi as her final destination. *Am I ready to do this?* The weight of her mission pressed on her chest again.

With many thoughts swirling in her head while gasping for some air, a friendly male voice fished her out of the depths of her mind, snapping Brenée back in line.

"Your boarding pass and ID, miss."

She froze for a moment, but with a spontaneous reflex, she handed the documents over to the agent. After verifying, the agent gave them back, "India, uh? Safe travels, miss!" Quietly, Brenée took them back in disbelief and continued walking forward. She was in.

Maybe I am ready. She thought, trying to gain some confidence.

Once through security, the airport terminal was a whirlwind of activity, with people rushing to and from, pulling their luggage and glancing at departure boards. The announcement system crackled with voices in English and Spanish, announcing departures and arrivals. The air was permeated with the distinctive blend of jet fuel, coffee, and the faint smell of fast food from the nearby concessions.

Finding a seat with her backpack by her side as her only companion, Brenée took a deep breath and glanced around desperately trying to find familiar faces. In a sea of people, she found none.

Reaching for her bag to fetch her mother's journal, she did as her mom instructed earlier, "Once you get to the airport, come back and see me," Hoping to calm her nerves, she opened the journal.

Hello, my Sunshine!

You are on your way to India.

I know this is a long trip, maybe one of the longest you will ever take. From your current location, you are about to embark on a journey of 8,000+ miles, and over 25 hours of estimated travel time. I understand you may be feeling nervous since it is your first time. That uneasiness will fade as you grow more comfortable navigating the unknown. So, if you feel that way, I assure you it is completely normal.

Also, Brenée, while the news often highlights the bad everywhere, experience has shown me that most people are nice, friendly, and kind. When you radiate positivity, good things will return to you. Remember the world around you is a mirror of your own reflection. Are you looking for the good or are you looking for the bad? Either way, you will find exactly that.

Don't be naïve, though. Be cautious, pay attention, and listen to your gut feeling for it is your internal compass - you know more than you think you do.

I will be providing more details once you're on the plane.

Oh, one last thing because I think you need to hear it again. You are not alone. I am here…traveling with you.

~Mom

Reading her mom's words came exactly at the right time. It was as if her mom knew what Brenée needed.

As the time for boarding drew near, she packed the journal and slung her backpack over her shoulders to walk toward the gate. Passing through boarding check, Brenée stepped onto the jet bridge, heading towards the aircraft that would carry her towards the far side of the world. With each step, the bridge swayed beneath her, just like her uneasy stomach.

Waiting for her turn again, Brenée held on to the plane door, reminding every single cell in her body there was no abyss underneath. *Am I ready to do this? Am I ready to do this?* She asked herself repeatedly.

Letting go of the plane door just like a dive into the sky, she took her first step.

Yes, I am!

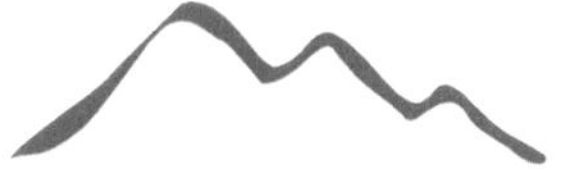

February 13th:
The Spiritual Bustle

Brenée sat on the window seat of a full flight alone and on her own. With the ashes in her bag and the journal in her hand, she knew her mom was now her only guide.

"Alright, mom. Here I am," Brenée opened the pages searching for more instructions.

Hello again,

Welcome to the beginning of an epic mission! India is magical, mystical and spiritual, but also intense. You will be challenged to find its beauty in the midst of hustle and bustle —noisy traffic every day, trash everywhere, and polluted air. If by now you haven't experienced culture shock…in India, I guarantee you will.

This is a place of contradictions with extreme poverty and gems of ancient wisdom coexisting under the same sky. Wherever you go, observe with no judgment, learn from people, and respect their culture.

Brenée paused from reading for a minute to wonder what was so magical about India given her mom's lukewarm description. This was certainly not a place she had ever been interested in visiting, but now, her curiosity was growing.

One more request - during my stay in India, I ate only vegetarian food and I'd like for you to do the same. You will appreciate the rich spices and flavors of India. It'll be good for you!

Trust me.

~Mom

Brenée closed the journal sharply, eyes wide open. Always a picky eater, this was a whole new layer to the challenge.

"Of course you had to make this more difficult, mom!" she nearly said it out loud, feeling like a child when asked to eat her veggies.

"Fine, mom. I will do it… I guess. Just for you," Brenée whispered to herself almost with a slight pout.

After three long flights and two layovers, the plane started descending through the clouds to her final destination. Brenée peered out of the window and her eyes filled with wonder and anticipation. The vast city of Delhi came into view with its vibrant colored buildings and sprawling landscapes offering a stunning contrast to the serene skies above.

The airplane wobbled gently as it made its final approach, and the hum of the engines filled the cabin. The landscape below shifted from a patchwork of fields and neighborhoods to a mesmerizing labyrinth of streets, buildings, and green spaces.

She could see the meandering Yamuna River, the lifeline of the city, and the red sandstone walls of the historic Red Fort in the distance, standing tall as a reminder of Delhi's past.

As the plane touched down on the runway, the wheels met the ground with a gentle thud and quickly decelerated. Brenée's heart raced with nervousness as the aircraft taxied to the gate. The flight attendant's announcement that they had landed in Delhi was followed by the cabin bursting with a mixture of murmurs, sighs of relief, and the rustle of seatbelts being unbuckled.

She could hardly contain her need to turn her cellphone back on to let her dad know she had landed. "I made it, dad." a short text let him know.

As she gathered her belongings, her movements seemed calm, but inside, adrenaline pumped through her veins to all corners of her body. Brenée felt her heartbeat almost to the speed of tribal drums while a variety of flying creatures from goose bumps to stomach butterflies took over her anatomy. Brenée looked out of the window one last time, taking in the view of the lively tarmac and the warm, golden sunlight. Although nervous, her tired body was ready to stretch and join the press of people walking their way down the aisle.

As she stepped off the plane and into the terminal, the slightly humid Delhi air felt different, filled with unfamiliar scents. Looking around, she spotted a clock stating the local time was 2:55 P.M. Just over 26 hours since she hugged her father goodbye.

The airport was bustling with people speaking in languages she didn't understand, yet the signs were conveniently in English too. Following the flow of travelers through the airport, she cleared customs and exited into the arrival hall.

Just one step before she reached the glass doors to exit the airport, Brenée stopped as she took in the scene. Standing amid unfamiliar faces with sharp loneliness, the intimidating world around her moved so quickly and she felt the need to halt. The weight of her solitude settled over her as she felt the reality that she was on the other side of the world…alone.

Doing her best to contain her tears, she pulled out her phone, trying to call her dad. As she started to dial the long numbers, she paused. *It's only 3:25 A.M. back home with the time difference. If I call dad right now, he will only worry and be alarmed.* She thought as she took a deep breath and remembered her mom's words: *"you are not alone. I am here…traveling with you."*

Taking another deep breath while straightening her shoulders, Brenée took the one step necessary to completely exit the overwhelming airport. As she started walking towards the busy sidewalk, her steps were cautious at first, but each following step felt a little more solid than the previous one. She stood up at the pickup area, raised her hand to hail a taxi, and the glossy, yellow-and-black cab soon pulled up to the curb. As she got in the back seat of the taxi, a soft, ambient Indian music played on the radio. The cab driver, a thin middle-aged man with a thick mustache, wore a simple white kurta and looked at Brenée in silence, clearly expecting directions.

As Brenée explained her destination, she realized he did not understand.

"I don't speak Hindi, but I need to go here to this hotel," Brenée said, and attempted to communicate by pointing at her phone map. The driver said something while squinting at the screen and shaking his head. She tried a few gestures and repeated the name of her destination louder as if the problem was his hearing, but still, it didn't click. The driver responded again in his language.

"I'm sorry. I…I don't understand," Brenée said in frustration as they were both lost in translation. "Thank you, but I will try another cab." Brenée couldn't open the cab door fast enough to subdue her growing anxiety.

Oh gosh, what am I going to do if I don't speak their language? Brenée nervously went back inside the airport, seeking some sense of refuge and shelter from the world.

Back in the arrival hall, right back to square one, Brenée sat on the floor against a wall with her knees pulled tight into her chest. Her body shivered and her face lost color to a mute pall. *What am I going to do? Did I fly all the way across the world for this, mom?* Brenée asked, draped in fear.

Almost like a subtle message speaking straight back to her, Brenée spotted an airline advertisement that felt much like an answer to her questions: *"Fly beyond your limits. The world awaits,"* her lips softly moved as she read again.

"Okay, mom. Yes, I hear you now."

Standing up, Brenée dusted herself off physically and figuratively. Picking up her backpack felt as if she was picking up her pieces to begin again.

She tried again, raising her hand out while standing on the curb to hail the next cab.

"Hello, do you speak English?" was Brenée's first question. After a friendly smile and a head nod, the driver said yes. A wave of relief washed over Brenée giving her face back her colors.

As she climbed in and gave him her destination, Brenée was set off into the spiritual bustle in the vibrant streets of India. She didn't know how her journey would end, but she knew it was about to start. The world was in fact awaiting.

February 14th:
Through the Forgotten Quest

The city's frenetic traffic quickly surrounded the cab as Brenée and the taxi driver pulled away in the car. Tuk-tuks, cars, and motorcycles weaved through the lanes, creating a dynamic and even somewhat insane symphony of movement and sounds. Towering billboards advertising everything from traditional saris to the latest smartphones covered the skyline. Brenée looked out the window feeling like a little girl, taking in the chaotic yet fascinating cityscape.

The taxi driver navigated the bustling streets with a skill and focus that can only be acquired with years of experience. He seemed to anticipate every sudden turn and merging lane while Brenée grew more captivated by the sights, sounds, and scents of Delhi with each passing kilometer.

She leaned back in the taxi seat noticing the bright tassels and shiny beaded strings dandling off the dashboard, while outside her window, Delhi unfolded around her. Street vendors selling colorful flowers, families on scooters, and the occasional sacred cow ambling along the roadside were some of the scenes Brenée marveled at. She was also faced, however, by the not-so-fascinating reality that her mom had talked about. Polluted air, a city overwhelmed by trash and nomad communities living under highways and bridges. Not to mention the heartbreaking sight of homeless families with babies lying on cribs made from newspaper. Before her eyes, Brenée was seeing poverty at a scale she had never experienced before.

This is going to be intense just as you said, mom, she thought to herself as she remembered her mom's words to keep an open mind and find beauty in the most unthinkable places.

The 30-minute journey from the airport to her hotel was an immersive introduction to the city's dynamic character. Upon arriving at the humble hotel her mom had chosen, Brenée felt an immense amount of gratitude for not having died as she traveled across the world.

Relocating her comfort zone to her hotel room, her energy plunged as she entered the room and spotted the bed covered with a colorful yet faded blanket.

Throwing her backpack down to the side, she flopped onto the bed.

"Ah! This feels amazing!" She exclaimed as she sank into the covers.

"I shouldn't get too comfortable, though," she continued. "I feel gross. I need a shower!"

Getting her body off the bed heavy with the weight of travel and her mind trapped between time zones, Brenée stepped into the bathroom as her eyes widened in confusion noticing something of great importance was missing – the toilet.

For a moment, she stood frozen, unsure of what was going on. Noticing a hole in the ground, Brenée glanced nervously stepping closer while avoiding being sucked in by what appeared to be as big as a black hole.

Confused about the strange setup, Brenée decided to turn around and go back to the front desk.

"Um, hi. I'm not sure what's going on, but there is no toilet in my bathroom. I think you gave me a room under construction," she said with obvious concern.

"Oh, no! You do have a toilet. It is a squat toilet," the friendly employee said in a business-as-usual tone, wobbling his head.

"So….you mean that I have to…squat down?" Brenée said clearly wanting to hear a different answer.

"Yes, correct," he replied.

With her mind racing to process the cultural difference, embarrassment washed over her as she realized she had no choice but to adjust to this completely unfamiliar arrangement. With a deep breath, she reminded herself that this was the hotel her mom recommended only hoping there was a good reason behind her plan.

"O-k-a-y. Thank you," Still the discomfort and culture shock lingered as she went back to her room trying to figure out how to navigate her new reality.

Very funny, mom! She thought as she walked away. *You forgot to mention this important piece of information!*

Back in her room, Brenée only had enough energy to take a shower and send a text message to her dad letting him know she had arrived safe and sound to her hotel.

Crawling into bed, she fell instantly asleep despite the distant honks from the bustling street outside and the occasional chatter in Hindi from staff and guests.

The next day, emerging from a deep, solid rest, Brenée woke up to the faint scent of cleaning sounds and smells drifting in from the room next door, where housekeeping was cleaning.

Feeling refreshed, Brenée could hardly wait to pull out her mother's journal curled up in her bed while she resumed reading after finding where she left off.

Welcome to India, my Sunshine!

During the following weeks, you will see a new reality, something you've never experienced before in America. Let me just say, my vision of life was not complete until I came here. This is a vibrant city with multiple things to offer, but the one that marked my heart for life came from visiting the forgotten streets in the slums of Delhi.

It was there that I came face-to-face with a picture of life I could never have imagined. When I first visited the slums, I spent an entire day with the children living there. I remember seeing fully built communities on top and around landfills. A clear vision of streams of sewage passing through the heart of the village along with the thick air with a mixture of unpleasant smells lingered in my mind for years. I remember houses built with various construction materials that on our side of the world would usually be considered scrap. But in the midst of all this, I remember above all, the children playing, smiling, and living in joy.

You may wonder, what were they so happy about?

Well, Brenée, they were happy simply with the pleasure of living.

It was as if their secret to happiness lay in the absence of material accumulations. I believe they experience the true essence of joy, that feeling which does not depend on material things. You see, Brenée, in the "civilized" world, we have been led to believe we need stuff to have joy. We have bought into the idea that the more stuff we have, the happier we are. And so, we learn to want more and expect more.

In truth, we don't need much to be happy.

It is the very act of wanting that can, in fact, be the root cause of unhappiness. I've found that happiness is freedom from wanting, a state of pure contentment and satisfaction with what you have. Only after understanding this simple concept will you realize why those children were purely and unconditionally happy.

They reminded me of a simple lesson I often forget: Happiness is complete non-attachment – freeing ourselves from emotional dependencies to outcomes, possessions and specific desires.

This is because attachment is often paired with a sense of fear of loss and ties to external factors for satisfaction. When we practice non-attachment, there is a greater acceptance of things as they are, experiencing a greater sense of peace, and finding joy in the moment rather than constantly seeking it in the future.

It is, therefore, my wish, Brenée, that you take me back to that place of pure joy and contented way of living to release part of me in the landfills.

"Wait. Release your ashes in the landfills?" Brenée opened her eyes wide to read the last sentence again. "You want me to do what? I traveled all the way to India to throw you in the trash?" Brenée exclaimed in shock, fighting with her mom about her insane idea. Her mom, anticipating her daughter's reactions, proceeded:

> Yes, you read that right. I chose the slums of Delhi as the first spot to release part of my ashes. Remember… happiness is non-attachment; happiness is letting go. You can't fill a cup if it is already full, so let's begin by making room. Don't forget, when you love the essence, the physical form does not matter anyway. So go ahead and spread my ashes in the land of waste.
>
> *~Mom*

Lying down in bed, Brenée closed the journal to process her mom's bizarre request. It took some time, but after a moment of reflection, she understood the purpose behind the slum quest. By releasing her ashes in the landfills, Brenée was to fulfill a true act of freedom, detachment, and letting go just as her mom had meant.

February 18th:
An Unfamiliar Image of Joy

After three days of building up the nerve to venture out to the slums, Brenée stood in the lobby of her hotel, holding a city map. Somewhere in Delhi were the settlements her mom talked about, but with vague directions, slow internet service, and a large percentage of the city covered by slums, she felt totally at a loss.

Approaching the front desk, she smiled nervously at the young male clerk. "Excuse me," she began. "Do you know how to get to this place?" Brenée pointed out the name written on a piece of paper.

"Madanpur Khadar," The clerk read looking at Brenée with a puzzled face. "You want to go there?" He asked curiously as Brenée responded with a head nod. "Um, it's really not hard, but it can be tricky as there are no street names in the village," he replied. He pulled out a map of the area and started drawing a path with his blue pen. "Go two kilometers north this way and then make a right turn here. Once you are to this corner, there will be a short stretch uphill where you will be able to spot the village," he said as he circled the location.

"Oh, so it is relatively close by," she realized after the clerk pointed out the distance.

"Yes, you can walk there. It will take about 35 minutes. Or…we could order a cab to take you there if you prefer," he replied.

"No way! I'm not walking there by myself. I prefer a cab," grateful, but still hesitant, Brenée asked one more question. "Let me ask you; is it safe for me to go there?"

"Um…as a precaution, I recommend visiting with someone local early in the day. I'm sure if you give the cab driver a good tip, he can go with you. He's a trustworthy man; his name is Aarav. We use his services all the time."

"That's a great idea! Could you make the arrangements for tomorrow morning please?" Brenée thanked the friendly clerk again and returned to her room, relieved to know she was not tackling the task alone.

Tomorrow, Mom. "We'll do it tomorrow, she thought as she tucked herself in bed anticipating the arrival of the day ahead.

The next morning tomorrow arrived. After introducing Aarav to Brenée, the drive to the slums started with the ashes carefully packed into her day bag.

In a matter of minutes, the cab drove for two kilometers north and then turned right to follow the map. Soon, they were going uphill spotting the village in the distance. Kilometer by kilometer, Brenée was heading towards a reality she had never been exposed to before. Here, the world looked very different.

The slums of Delhi were an unembellished departure from the more polished parts of the city into the narrow maze of makeshift dwellings. Built from a mix of corrugated metal, weathered plywood, and tarpaulin, these communities formed a chaotic, yet strangely organized puzzle of poverty.

As they parked and entered the village, Brenée experienced a kaleidoscope of complex sights, sounds, and smells –vibrant colorful laundry hanging on clotheslines waved beside fly-infested open sewers with decaying smells coming from all directions.

"Phew!" Brenée waived her hand and covered her nose; "Whoa!" she said as she swiftly reacted to steer clear of the tangled web of electric wires and cables.

It was a world of sharp contrasts, where she navigated the intricate alleyways with caution.

At the near distance right on top of the garbage hills, there they were - the children her mom talked about. Commonly known in India as the "rag-pickers," the children dug through the piles of waste collecting anything and everything of value to eat or sell.

With Aarav in close proximity, Brenée slowly climbed towards the children. Her heart became heavier as she estimated the rag-pickers were children under the age of twelve. Their faces smeared with dirt, but their eyes sparked with curiosity as they saw Brenée.

"Hi," she waived her hand to greet them. The children responded with a smile as they kept their hands busy digging through the trash. Touched by the scene, Brenée felt an immediate need to give. Reaching into her bag, she took out of the side pocket some chocolate cookies and offered them to the children squatting down on bare feet. Before she knew it, she was surrounded by many little hands begging for a cookie.

"Whooo! Hold on, children!" she exclaimed as she looked for more snacks to share. "I'm sorry! I have no more cookies. I'm truly sorry," Brenée said as she showed the empty wrappers. One by one, the children went back to picking through the garbage in search of more treasures to find.

Their innocent laughter provided an emotional counterpoint to the harsh conditions in which they lived. Perhaps, that was the sound of the astounding feeling of joy that her mom talked about despite the lack of financial provisions.

The pure joy you talked about, mom. I feel it. Yet, I'm not sure I quite understand it, she thought as she listened to the children work and play while sharing the struggles of the day. Although this was unfamiliar to her, Brenée could not help but feel admiration for their resilience at such young age.

As she continued her walk through the slums with Aarav by her side, Brenée came across a small one-story building that had a sign outside in Hindi. "Aarav, is that a school?" She asked her unofficial tour guide.

"Yes, it is," he replied.

"Um, I'm sure this is the elementary school mom visited when she came to India," Brenée sensed it instinctively, remembering pictures of her mom with the children. Drawn to the school, she approached the building like she was looking for a piece of her mother inside. With caution, Brenée took a quick peek into the room.

There was a hallway leading to three rooms with no doors clearly visible from where she stood. One room had a computer in the corner. The antique piece of technology had a round monitor - one of those which had been outdated for decades. In the other two rooms, which appeared to be classrooms, children were sitting on the floor covering the room from wall to wall.

After seeing Brenée, who for obvious reasons didn't seem to belong, a teacher came up to her asking a question that Brenée didn't understand.

"I'm sorry, ma'am. Do you speak English?" The petite teacher, wearing a traditional Hindu outfit with a red dot between her eyebrows, made a hand signal asking Brenée to wait. A few minutes later, the same teacher showed up with another lady who spoke English.

"Namaste," the lady of glasses, dressed in an emerald-green saree bowed with kindness as she greeted Brenée. "I'm the principal of this school. How can I help you?" the lady asked.

Brenée returning the kind gesture, greeted her back honoring their customs.

"Namaste, ma'am. My name is Brenée and I'm traveling from America. My mom volunteered to come to India years ago on a Seva trip (service trip) and this is one of the settlements she visited. Mom would tell stories of the deep sense of connection she felt to the children of this area and from the only school in the village. She wanted me to pay a visit again. I believe this is the school. Is this it? Is this the only school in this community?" Brenée asked.

"Yes, this is it. Come, come!" the principal invited her in as Brenée released an exhale she hadn't realized she was holding.

"Is your mom with you?" she asked looking for someone else to be with her.

"No, it's just me. Oh, and this is Aarav; he's keeping me company today," Brenée explained.

"So, are you traveling through India as a volunteer as well?" the principal asked.

"Well, not exactly. Um, I know this is going to sound unusual," Brenée paused for a moment to find the right words to explain. "My mom passed away six months ago," she felt a big lump in her throat. "I'm scattering her ashes at places that held special significance to her. Those were her last wishes, and I am honoring them. That's the reason why I'm here." Brenée concluded on the verge of tears.

"I'm sorry to hear that," the woman made a face of compassion as she placed both hands on her chest. "As for her final wishes, they are not unusual. They are beautiful," she added.

"Mom asked me to specifically come to this village. She said this place gave her a complete vision of the world, which is why she chose it as one of her resting places."

"Well, your mother was right. Visiting this place is such an eye-opening experience. You get to see the reality of poverty first-hand and hopefully feel inspired to take social responsibility and action.

You see, this very second, millions of people are facing serious struggles and challenges; struggles non-existent to those who live a life of privilege and comfort. We are talking about the lack of access to food, clean water, fresh air, and education – basic necessities all humans have. There are vast systemic wealth, and inequality issues the people are facing. By coming here, you get to see a reality most people want to forget about, and others totally ignore. I have been a principal of this school for five years now," she said, "as an educator, I feel a strong sense of responsibility to not only acknowledge but also contribute towards a positive change on future generations."

Brenée felt the heaviness of the principal's words that spoke of a sad reality.

"Want to know something?" The principal adjusted her glasses, "we have been looking for someone to teach basic English words to the children…and now you show up. No pressure, but if interested, I would like to extend an invitation for you to teach to the children for a week. That would give you a great opportunity to do Seva, just like your mom did years ago and give us more time to find a permanent teacher. So, what do you say?"

Brenée looked at her with certain confusion, "Just like that? I mean that sounds great, but…no ID, no background check, no forms to fill out?" she asked surprised by the simplicity of the offer.

"Brenée, look around," the lady made a gesture inviting her to take a look, "There is nothing you can take from us because we already have nothing. Besides," she continued, "I see your soul through your eyes, and I can tell you're a sweet young lady. I can also see you're still mourning."

In the spontaneity of the moment, Brenée threw herself into the principal's arms in a sincere hug. "Thank you! I'm sure this is what my mom would have wanted. She loved to serve while she had the chance."

That day, Brenée did not only visit the slums of Delhi like her mom did years ago but unexpectedly stepped into the role of Seva as a teacher, contributing to the unfamiliar image of joy.

February 24th:
Gold in the Landfills

S tanding in front of the mirror, Brenée pulled her hair back into a ponytail smoothing down the loose strands as she watched her reflection in the glass. She wore a modest blouse and a simple skirt to look at least somewhat professional. Though her wardrobe was limited, her heart swelled with an unlimited surge of eagerness and anticipation.

After an introduction from the principal to the big group, she was left to begin her teachings. The young learners, ranging between the ages of 5 to 10, sat on colorful floor mats while she held flashcards with pictures on them. "DOG," Brenée pointed to the image and slowly enunciated the word "dog," encouraging the children to repeat after her. Some children participated with exaggerated pronunciation, while others were shyly looking down and glancing at each other. "CAT," she said as some children were giggling and others acting silly.

Brenée smiled often, trying to keep the energy positive, occasionally giving a thumbs-up or a gentle nod of encouragement whenever they would get a word right. Despite her inexperience, Brenée quickly connected with her students and fell in love with them almost immediately.

Then, after school hours, Brenée would join the teachers and students to tend to the school grounds. They would start by splitting the big team into smaller groups to pick up garbage in the areas surrounding the building.

Even when the garbage collection task seemed quite impossible, almost senseless, they did the work.

The seven days volunteering at the school in the slums slipped by in what felt as an instant.

On her last day teaching, Brenée walked to the hotel lobby ready as usual at 7:15 A.M.

"Are you waiting on your taxi driver, Miss? The hotel clerk asked.

"No, not anymore. Today, I'm walking to the slums on my own. It's only a 35-minute walk," she smiled as she began her last journey to the village.

After her last English lesson to the children, Brenée sat outside the building feeling nostalgic and helpless. Noticing in the distance, the principal walked towards her, sitting down next to the young woman.

"I think your job here is done, Brenée," she said.

"But I feel like I did so little," Brenée said, heartbreak in her voice.

"That's not true! You came here to make a difference in the lives of each child. What you did is remarkable.

Tell me, how many of your friends volunteer their time to help those in need?" Brenée shook her head no in silence.

"But, do you think the children will have the opportunity to continue learning English? Will they keep this place clean on their own? Look at the amount of trash we've collected, yet we're still surrounded by piles of more! Picking up trash practically felt as if we were carrying buckets of water out of the ocean," Brenée said with clear frustration, pointing to the landfills surrounding them.

"Brenée," the principal interrupted in a passive tone. "Our school educates about eighty children per year. Most parents do not send their children to school as they'd rather send them out to the landfills to pick through the garbage. To them, school is a waste of time that takes them away from survival duties. Life in the slums is all they know and, more than likely, this is all they will ever know. However, because we know better, we continue doing our duty with no expectations. We do the work because if we can positively influence the life of one child out of eighty, that is enough for us. Positive change starts with one person choosing to do the right thing, even when it looks pointless."

"Mm, I think I know what you are saying," Brenée said. "I believe that's what mom was trying to tell me. That happiness is living a life of non-attachment, a life with no expectations. Expectation is the root of disappointment and therefore, unhappiness," Brenée's realization sank a little deeper.

The principal chimed in, nodding in agreement.

"Look Brenée, we do our work out of love without expecting anything from the children. We teach the children to choose education over ignorance, care over chaos. When you ask if they will continue studying or maintaining this place clean, the answer is maybe, maybe not. That should not stop us, however, from teaching them the value of education and cleanliness."

The principal paused for a moment and took a deep breath as she looked out over the slums that surrounded them.

"Did you know, Brenée, that a core belief in Hinduism is the idea of Karma Yoga; we fulfill our Dharma (duty) without attachment to the results. We focus on our actions rather than the fruits of them. In a Universe where everything is in constant change, expectations are often rigid, setting up a conflict with the flow of life. When things inevitably don't go as expected, it causes stress and unhappiness because we resist accepting change, the natural state of life. However, life itself is in a constant state of motion." Brenée listened not to respond, but to understand as the principal continued.

"By recognizing and releasing expectations – if the children will continue their education or keeping this place clean – you can achieve a more peaceful and content state of mind, free from disappointment. Do you know what I mean, Brenée?"

Brenée whispered, "Yes, I think I understand now. I think the children are so happy because they don't have expectations or attachments to anything. They are truly free."

As Brenée stood up getting ready to leave, the principal stopped her momentarily, "Brenée, we have a surprise for you," the principal yelled something in Hindi and the children gathered around her to give her hugs and shower her with gratitude. Following Hindu tradition, they draped multiple garlands of fresh yellow jasmines around her neck. With orange paint on her index finger, the principal put a bindi (dot) between Brenée's eyebrows.

"Go on, Brenée, and whatever your hands find to do, do it in dedication to your own supreme self-realization and in accordance with universal law. Remember to take peace wherever you go and in stillness, let it grow." Brenée gently closed her eyes as the principal tapped her forehead.

"Don't forget about us," one little girl said to Brenée. "Trust me. That is impossible," Brenée replied desperately struggling to keep her emotions from spilling over.

"Goodbye, children!" Brenée walked backwards waving at the children and teachers, savoring the view to the last second.

"Goodbye, Brenée!" a chorus of tiny voices rang out with cheerful goodbyes, filled with innocence and affection.

Eventually, when it was not possible to go backwards anymore, she turned around leaving the school behind to continue on.

Alone once again, Brenée found herself climbing a winding trail through the landfills. From the top, she could see out over the vast expanse of garbage, with its pungent and obnoxious odors. The gloomy landscape was a chaotic mix of discarded items, waste, and a sea of plastic containers of various kinds. However, in the middle of this depressing scene, Brenée freed her mind and saw a surreal beauty filtered through layers of smog and dust where the vibrancy of nature was both muted and intensified by the urban grit. Before her bare eyes, a sunset appeared dimmed by a layer of thick polluted air, allowing her to gaze at it without squinting. Amazed by the deep hues of burnt orange and purplish gray, she could almost hear her mom whispering in her ear that in India, it was possible for beauty to exist among the waste.

Receiving, one by one, the teachings the slums offered, Brenée reached deep into her bag to carefully take her mother's ashes out, cradling the urn between her hands.

"Mom, I'm sure you are proud of my Seva and efforts to make this a better place. Now before I leave, I'm doing what you asked for." Brenée's eyes glistened with tears as she opened the lid, exposing the ashes of her beloved mom. As irrational as it seemed, Brenée extended her arm to slowly scatter part of the precious dust on the unpleasant landfills.

Under a hazy sunset, Brenée felt a curtain being pulled back to fill a darkened room with light. In that moment, she saw with renewed eyes the real essence of beauty, going far beyond what the world taught her. Right there in the landfills, Brenée let go of something as precious as gold enveloped in a sunset of blur and glow.

February 26th:
A Million Diamonds

The following day, the instructions were for Brenée to pack her traveler's bag and continue her journey to Rishikesh. It was early in the morning when she took the day-long train ride up north leaving behind the busyness, the noise, and the chaos of Delhi.

As the train departed, the scenery shifted from urban sprawl to lush green fields and villages. The air also grew fresher, and a soft blue sky was revealed once again.

Her mom described that Rishikesh was a beautiful small town nestled in the lap of the Himalayas, situated along the banks of the sacred river Ganges. The town was renowned as the capital of yoga and regarded as one of the holiest towns of India.

Upon arrival, Brenée instantly understood why her mom wanted to make this town her second place of rest. Perhaps it was the old temples of weathered stone steps and carved doorways sitting upon the verdant slopes of the Himalayas or the beautiful bright sunlight reflecting on the abundant waters of the Ganges. Maybe it was the foot bridge suspended over the river moving to the rhythm of the wind, or simply the fresh, breathable air that was lacking in Delhi.

Brenée didn't know which part her mom liked the best, but one thing was for sure; time felt as if it could be stopped in Rishikesh.

As her mom instructed, Brenée was to stay at a well-known ashram in Rishikesh, the same ashram she stayed at. When she arrived, Brenée had no idea what an ashram was, but as she walked the paths, she began to grasp what her mom had described: This was a secluded place providing retreat to those seeking spiritual growth while practicing yoga and meditation.

Characterized by simplicity and modesty, the ashram provided only the bare minimum essentials that would cover Brenée's basic needs. Sharing the room with two other female visitors, Brenée entered her assigned space, which included a single bed, a quilted blanket, and a wooden chair.

"Namaste," Brenée said, having by now embraced this common greeting to say hello to others.

"Namaste," one of the girls replied, momentarily pausing what she was doing. "My name is Lucia and I'm from California."

"I'm Daniela," the other woman said. "I come from Greece."

"Nice to meet you both, I'm Brenée and I'm from Texas."

"Well, welcome, Brenée!" Lucia said warmly, inviting Brenée to make herself comfortable in her new space.

"First time in Rishikesh?" Daniela asked.

"Yes, first time in India actually. And truth be told, I had no idea what an ashram was," Brenée said, face blushing slightly with embarrassment.

"Oh, I hear you. When I first visited India, I had no idea either. Now, it's my second time here in this ashram and I think you will love it," Lucia said.

"Sorry to be so brief but we were on our way out to catch a yoga class. Please get settled and if you need anything, just let us know," Daniela said.

"Thank you! Enjoy your class," Brenée replied and then abruptly remembered. "Oh wait! Yes, one question before you leave!" Brenée said with a sense of urgency. "I just have to know – is there a regular toilet in this room or a hole in the ground?" Both girls laughed, and Brenée flashed a nervous smile.

"No, no hole in the ground! We have a regular toilet. The bathroom is to your right," Daniela pointed out.

"Oh, thank goodness!" Brenée replied with a big smile on her face. "That's all I needed to know!"

After she finished unpacking, Brenée headed out to explore the ashram. It was filled with winding trails through beautiful gardens, which invited her to wander in the serenity of nature.

Even when all alone, Brenée realized she didn't feel lonely. Her heart was so full; it felt as if her mom was walking right alongside her.

"Oh, this is so beautiful!" Brenée marveled at the gurgling fountains that captured her attention. "Oh, look at that!" Brenée admired the ornately decorated gate adorned with traditional Hindu symbols signifying purity and divinity. "Interesting!" she exclaimed passing several deity statues, which were placed in niches along the walls. Enjoying these quiet conversations with her mom about the beauty of the ashram, she was interrupted by her stomach grumbling loudly. Laughing at the sound, it drew her back to the present. Realizing she had been walking on an empty stomach, she checked her watch to see the time.

"Oh, shoot! It's 5:20 P.M. and dinner is only served through 6!" She said out loud, remembering the housekeeping instructions upon arrival.

Rushing to avoid missing dinner, she found her way back to the heart of the ashram to locate the Annapurna Hall, the community dining space, and slipped into line. With only a few other people in front of her, she noticed everybody taking their shoes off as they entered the communal space and then sitting on the floor to eat.

Following their lead, Brenée removed her shoes and grabbed a tray with both hands. Without menu options, every single person got the only one meal of the day, which was Palak Paneer with a piece of naan. Quite intrigued by the vibrant green dish, Brenée's eyes were wide with curiosity. She had never seen anything quite as green as this. Before her was a bright emerald sauce of creamy texture, dotted with soft, white cubes. The aroma was new to her, a blend of spices that tickled her nose, and despite the uncertainty, it made her mouth water.

She hesitated, unsure of what to make of this unfamiliar meal. With her eyes focused on her food, she managed to find a spot to sit on the floor. Bringing her focus back to the green dish, her fingers inched forward to poke at one of the cubes. The cube jiggled. With a deep breath, she scooped up a tiny piece with the naan. She took a tentative bite of the creamy sauce and her expression slowly shifted from uncertainty to delight. She beamed as the rich, savory flavors of spinach and cubed paneer filled her mouth, already reaching for more. Soon, her plate was empty.

After dinner, Brenée's stomach was quite content, and she decided to set out to continue exploring the gardens. By then, the clock ticked past 6:45 P.M. and the sunset was announcing its rapid arrival. In the distance, she heard traditional Hindu music, which got louder with every step she took towards the river.

Drawn by the music, she followed the sound down a trail towards Mother Ganga, as known by the locals. As she approached the source of the music, she paused, taking in the sight of a large crowd gathered along the riverbank, seated on the ground chanting, swaying, and clapping to the rhythm of the melodies. The songs were performed by young monks dressed in vibrant orange robes using strange instruments Brenée had certainly never seen before. But even when she couldn't understand the music, the lyrics, or the instruments, one thing was certain - she wanted to be part of this devotional ritual.

With a bright red-orange sunset slowly hiding behind the jagged Himalayas, Brenée rushed to join the crowd after taking her shoes off and finding a spot to sit down by the river.

Clapping to the meditative music and the flowing sounds of water, she listened with depth, swaying side to side to the cyclical, almost hypnotic, repetitive phrases that built upon each other. Brenée found herself in a tranquil, reflective state.

In this sublime moment, the sun's rays dazzled like a million diamonds on the water while the motherly river bathed Brenée with its fluid love. Closing her eyes and opening all her senses, Brenée felt the devotional songs turned to poetry for her soul. Transcending the boundaries of language and words, the emotional depth and spiritual essence of the music were palpable, making it a profound, heartfelt moment unlike anything experienced before.

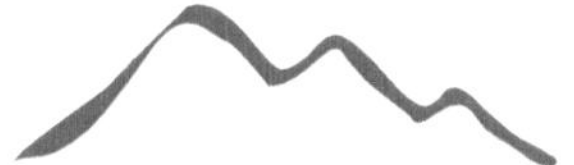

March 1st:
To Be Water, To Be Flow

Over the next few days, Brenée woke up early to attend a variety of spiritual adventures ranging from yoga with her roommates to meditation with the rishis and sages. Other times, Brenée would go for slow walks on the narrow roads of Rishikesh to visit a quaint café located on the other side of town. Though it was quite a walk, the café was a subtle reminder of home, making the trek worthwhile just to relax in a cozy corner, connect to Wi-Fi, and video call her dad. She was surprised to realize how much her homesickness had faded, yet it was always comforting to reconnect with her dad back home.

As she felt more confident navigating the small town, she embarked on her biggest adventure yet: crossing the Ganga River by walking on the slim and lengthy suspension bridge, which connected the East and the West parts of town over the flowing waters.

One of those mornings, as she stood at the edge of the swaying structure, Brenée reached into the depths of her soul for the courage to take her first step. Her palms turned sweaty as she gripped the worn rope railing. The bridge, made of old wooden planks with gaps between them, was not only crossed by foot explorers, but also by the loud traffic of scooters and wild monkeys hanging off the bridge wires.

Stepping onto this unconventional highway with a diverse variety of travelers, Brenée's heart pounded in her chest with every step forward. She felt the planks beneath her feet tremble with the intensified vibrations of the shaking structure. "Beep, beep" another scooter zipping by warned Brenée with a sharp, high-pitched sound to move out of the way. Beads of sweat streamed down her forehead with a blend of fear and determination. Taking deep breaths, Brenée focused on the other end of the bridge, where she knew solid ground awaited, instead of the rushing current beneath her feet.

But even in heart-pounding moments like crossing an old, suspended bridge, Brenée gained valuable insights from this and other adventures.

One of the simplest yet most memorable lessons she learned in Rishikesh came from a homeless man. One afternoon, while walking back to the ashram from crossing the river, Brenée's usual unpaved path was blocked by bricks, rocks and orange cones, signaling road closures. Unsure of any other way to return and with no internet signal, she began to worry.

Oh gosh, what am I going to do now? I only know one way back to the ashram! She thought in panic as she could see her destination within sight.

A man living in the streets sitting nearby observed her dilemma and called out her attention, waving his arm making a gesture. Brenée noticed, but she didn't pay attention. The man insisted. Moving his arm from left to right in an upward curved motion, Brenée stopped to watch him as she began to mimic the sign.

His message was delivered: Jump over. Keep going.

Like a sudden spark of realization, Brenée shifted her gaze back to the various obstacles and noticed how low they were to the ground. What initially seemed like a towering mountain blocking the road was now an easy step over bricks and stones. With the same simplicity the homeless man saw the solution, Brenée jumped over, thanked the man, and kept going.

That afternoon as the sunset covered the Himalayas in golden tones, Brenée sat by the banks of the Ganga still thinking about the wise old man. In a flash of clarity, Brenée opened her mind to the grasp that many of the worries she carried were not even real, and that, more often than not, the solution was as simple as jumping over it and moving forward.

Mom, Brenée thought, *I wish you could see how much I have grown. I am now learning to be flexible like water – fluid when warm and solid when cold. I believe this is the perfect time to do this.*

With the Ganga River flowing abundantly before her eyes, Brenée opened the ash container with a tilt to the right and extended her arm to let the gentle breeze carry some.

"Mom, you have grown too," she said out loud," Now, you have become a river, a perfect mirror to the sky. Go on and gracefully flow.

Dance through the land and whisper secrets to the rocks," Brenée said, watching the ashes drift away.

At the end of a beautiful day under a glowing sunset, Brenée had meaningful reflections as she celebrated both their growth. Brenée not only fulfilled her mother's desires to be water, but also to be river, to be flow.

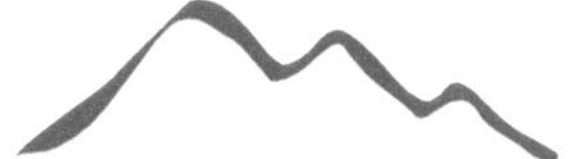

March 4th:
Romana's Garden

F our sunsets later, Brenée settled into the verdant sanctuary of the ashram, where blossoms and leaves dripped from tangled vines and opened her mom's journal to lose herself in the pages.

Hello, my Sunshine!

I hope your stay in the ashram has been peaceful and meaningful like it was for me years ago. Before you leave this town, I would love for you to travel to the northern part of Rishikesh to visit an orphanage called Romana's Children Garden.

This place was founded by an American lady from Colorado, who left the comfort of a civilized country to pursue a bold goal – she opened an orphanage in India.

Very few people are willing to do what she did.

Learn from her story, learn about her, and if you can, be of service to her mission.

The orphanage, the children, and you will all benefit from it.

Love,

~Mom

The following morning, Brenée left the ashram as instructed, weighted down by her backpack yet with an uplifted spirit.

With "north" as her single and main point of reference, Brenée walked uphill for 40 minutes in search of the orphanage. Following signs and asking the locals walking by, she knew she had found it when she saw a large wooden sign, battered by the elements that read: "Welcome to Romana's Children Garden."

Located close to a cliff in the Himalayas, Brenée opened the iron gates of the orphanage, and was instantly greeted by a well-defined path that took her through farming fields of various green kinds. Unlike most places she had seen in India thus far, this one was strikingly clean and amazingly organized.

For a minute, she felt as if she had stepped into a place that would only exist in the fantasy land of hobbits and fantasy tales.

Scattered in the lavish fields were round adobe huts built with river stones and broken glass to reflect natural light. The path had many ups and downs, bends and turns, lefts and rights as Brenée walked along. "Organic Café," a colorful wooden sign led the way.

Café! I must go, she thought, as a tinge of home sickness stirred - a tender memory of her dad waiting for her at the end of the road before reaching the final turn.

Once at the Café, Brenée opened the heavy wooden door studded with rusted iron nails and stepped into a magical space. Large, round windows let in the sunlight and colorful crystal ornaments hanging from the ceiling added to the charm. Stretching from wall to wall, Brenée spotted a long, low communal table surrounded by mustard and fuchsia decorative pillows on the floor for comfortable seating. Taking in the enchanting scene, her face lit up with awe.

"Hello! Welcome to Romana's Café. Is it just you today?" a young lady with an Australian accent interrupted Brenée's observations.

"Hi, well...yes. It's only me, but I'm here to find out how I can become a volunteer. Do you think you can help me?" Brenée asked.

"Oh, okay. Yes! You need to go to the main office," the woman responded with a smile. "You take an immediate left here and continue until you see the purple wooden sign to the main office. It should be open right now. What kind of volunteer work would you like to do?"

"Well, my family owns coffee shops back home. I know how to roast coffee, attend the coffee bar, and manage the cash register," Brenée promptly responded. "I can also prepare easy meals," she added with a smile.

"Sounds amazing! More hands are always needed here. Go talk to them," the young employee said.

"Thank you, I appreciate it. Hopefully I'll see you around!" Brenée replied.

Brenée's energy buzzed with excitement as she walked into the main office. The room immediately drew her eye with its numerous pictures of smiling children hugging a woman with long gray hair and wrinkles of age defining her face.

"Hello, how can I help you?" a lady sitting behind the desk asked.

"Um, Hi! My name's Brenée and I am traveling through India. My mom came here years ago, and I believe she met the woman in the pictures when she visited." Brenée pointed at the framed images hanging off the walls.

"That was the founder of this place," the coordinator replied. "She died a few years ago. So, you said your mom met her?" she asked with a smile on her face.

"Yes, she did. My mom was deeply moved by her story," Brenée continued. "She spoke of this orphanage as a magical place; she saw how loved the children were and knew she had to contribute. In fact, three weeks after she came home, she raised money for this place at our church and now she has asked me to come here to volunteer my time."

"Well, I'm glad you're here. We can certainly use your help!" the woman replied. "Let me give you a formal introduction of this place," the lady stood up to walk towards the nearest window. "Romana's Garden provides shelter, nutritious foods, and education to more than 200 children. In our fields, we grow our own vegetables and fruits to feed the children and sell at our Café. Everything we produce is healthy and organic. Volunteering duties range from helping the children study, taking them out to play, helping cook their meals, or attend the Café," she said proudly. "What duties are you interested in doing and how long are you staying here for?"

"I can volunteer for 2 to 3 weeks," Brenée said. "As for what I can do, at home I work at my family's coffee shops. If possible, I'd like to work at your Café."

"How would you like to work in the kitchen to cook for the children? We always need an extra set of hands there to cook three meals every day. Also, we ask volunteers to commit to a month minimum. Can you do that?"

"In the main kitchen for a month, huh?" Brenée paused to think about the volunteer expectations. "Yes, why not? When do you need me to start?" Brenée made the spontaneous decision on the spot.

"Wonderful! We're glad to have you," the woman officially welcomed Brenée. "You can begin tomorrow if that works for you," The woman went on to explain, "Living conditions here are basic. You will receive what you need such as lodging, healthy meals, and clean water. We ask you to pay ₹800 rupees for the month, which is the equivalent of $130 dollars to cover all expenses. You will be sharing rooms with other volunteers as needed. Also, know that you will be a role model to the children, so you are required to express yourself and behave accordingly. No drugs, alcohol, or cigarettes are allowed either." As she went over the details, she handed Brenée some forms to sign.

"Here's the paperwork required to be completed and signed," she said.

"Ah forms! You need me to fill out forms," Brenée said with a chuckle.

"Is that a problem?" the lady asked.

"No, not at all!" A smile stretched crossed her face as she unwrapped the memory of the slum.

Thousands of miles away from home, Brenée felt a familiar comfort – clean space, drinking water, and yes…necessary forms.

March 20th:
A Green Awakening

“This is your bedroom, Brenée. Make yourself at home,” the coordinator said as she opened the door to the room. “You will stay by yourself until we get another female volunteer. If you need anything, let me know. The weather is expected to turn tonight so you can grab additional blankets from the linen closet inside the laundry room.” She pointed at a stand-alone room across the fields.

“You will need to report to Emilie in the kitchen tomorrow at 7 A.M. Emilie is the one in charge there. She’s a volunteer from Norway. She joined us two years ago and has been a wonderful blessing to this place. I am sure you will get along with her and the rest of the team just fine.”

“Great! I can’t wait to work with them,” Brenée said, dropping her backpack down onto her new headquarters. After exchanging a few more words, Brenée settled down in her new room and called her dad to share the news of the day.

Reporting to Emilie the next day, Brenée met the seven volunteers she was to work with. They were visiting from places Brenée had never even heard of before – Bergen, Norway; Lübeck, Germany; Delft, Netherlands to name a few.

During her time at Romana’s Garden, Brenée learned to wear many hats, perform various skills, and take on different responsibilities.

She loved getting up early with the morning sun warming her face to pick the vegetables to be used for the day. Her hands were small, but her technique was effective - she would kneel in the garden, grab the leafy green top, and pull in one strong motion, making a bright orange carrot appear over the soil.

Nearby, plump tomatoes and crisp lettuce waited to be collected and added to her basket. Once her basket got full, she would go back inside the kitchen to start making a garden salad topped with walnuts and drizzled with virgin olive oil to accompany the children's main meals.

It was hard for her to believe the shifts she'd had in her own perspective. Brenée had gone from thinking eating only vegetables was unpleasant to being the one picking a vegetable, looking at it and thinking of the possibility of creating hearty meals.

It was there, at Romana's Organic Garden, during a science class she attended with the children that she learned about the importance of eating less meat. Not only were vegetarian meals good for the body, but also, they were good for the environment. She learned that as demand for meat grows, agriculture's emissions rise, steadily polluting the environment. Brenée was exposed to the sad reality that unless people change their eating habits to eat less meat and more vegetables, the situation could become more extreme and dramatic for future generations. Working at this orphanage not only opened Brenée's eyes to a new level of awareness, but she also felt moved to do something about it.

Mom, Brenée wrote a side note on her mom's journal. *I now appreciate more the reason why you would eat meat occasionally and why you thought it was important for me to embrace vegetarian eating while here. After over a month in India, I do not miss meat. I have learned how to cook with aromatic spices, fresh herbs and colorful vegetables. Thank you!*

Beyond fresh food, Brenée realized she was reaping the benefits of clean air and the hands-on work outdoors – an energizing contrast to hours spent behind a computer, phone, or studying within four walls. She was immersed in nature, and the culture of growing a garden, tending the land and caring for the orphans. That awakened something within her, the exact feeling that perhaps her mom intended to pass down to her.

That afternoon, beneath the golden glow of the sunset, Brenée felt a green awakening lavishly blossoming with gratitude for being more aware and more educated than the day before.

March 26th:
The Missing Piece Found

Volunteering at the orphanage flew by in an instant. Brenée would work day in and day out, helping cook for the children and attending to them along with the team. She loved getting tight warm hugs from the children and looking at their big eyes after serving them hot delicious meals at the dining hall.

It had been 41 sunsets in India, more than she ever planned for, and Brenée's visit was soon coming to an end.

The day came that she needed to say goodbye and continue the path designed by her mom.

I will miss this place so much, mom, Brenée thought as she connected with her mom in her mind. She was savoring the last moments at the orphanage, overlooking the land she'd tended and a group of children playing ball in the distance. A girl, leaving her friends behind, dashed toward Brenée and wrapped her in a tight hug. "I'll miss you so much, Brenée," she said.

"I'll miss you too!" echoed another girl, running over.

In no time, the children were expressing how much they would miss Brenée.

"Nooo! I will miss you the most, kids," Brenée sucked in a deep breath. "You gave me so much when I needed it the most. Truly, I will miss you more." Deep inside, Brenée felt like an orphan too without her mom.

"Thank you, Brenée," Emilie joined the group. "You are so patient and kind. If you ever become a mom, you will be a great one."

"Thank you, Emilie," Brenée said, feeling deeply moved by her words. "The truth is I didn't know I liked children so much until I came here to India."

"Well, now you know that among all the many gifts you have, you have the gift of connecting with children. I am sure you will make something of that." Emilie smiled as Brenée found herself once again saying goodbyes and walking away from a place she'd come to love.

Yet even when leaving, she knew she'd left her own lasting footprints behind.

Following the farewell to the orphanage, Brenée made her way back to the sacred Ganga. She wanted to take in the view of the river and enjoy the soothing sounds of the flowing water gracefully running by the foot of the Himalayas one last time.

Dressed in a royal blue top and a comfortable long skirt with sandals, she did not hesitate to step into the water. Facing the majestic river, she began to walk in immersing her body step by step in the crystal-clear waters.

Standing tall covered up to her chest, Brenée took a deep breath and, in one motion, dipped her head and shoulders – getting completely submerged in the sacred waters. Brenée performed this ritual as a symbol of enlightenment as she embraced a refreshed mindset.

Without a doubt, India was an intense, magical, and beautiful place just like her mom had described. Her mom said India was the missing piece to attain a complete view of the world and now Brenée understood the full meaning of her words.

In the midst of poverty and waste, Brenée found the missing piece - and with that, the puzzle was complete.

March 28th:
Whispers of the Future

Aboard the train heading back to Delhi, Brenée sat with her mom's journal in her hands, "where to now, mom?" she asked with a twinkle in her eyes lit with anticipation. She was a little nervous as she opened the journal but mostly elated like standing at the edge of something wonderful with the wind at her back.

Hello, my Sunshine!

As your travels through India come to an end, I thank you for bringing me back to this mystical place.

Now, it's time to continue the journey and catch a flight to the land of tapas and Gaudí: Barcelona.

Barcelona is like a dream painted in warm colors. The buildings aren't just walls – they are stories carved in stone. Gaudi's creations twist and swirl like something out of a fairy tale, and the streets in the Gothic Quarter feel like stepping back in time. But the best part? The city hums with life. You can hear music drifting from open windows, smell fresh bread from tiny bakeries, and taste the salt in the air as you walk along the beach.

It is utterly astonishing. This is the day you will see it for yourself.

Happy travels!

~Mom

"Spain, huh?! Mom wants to go to Spain next!" Brenée whispered to herself while the rhythmic rattle of the iron wheels echoed through the train carriage. Closing the journal in one snap, she started making plans for the next mission landing on her lap.

It was early Thursday morning when Brenée woke up in Delhi to catch her flight to Spain. She felt a deep uneasiness – a very similar kind of feeling she had when her mom left. It was as if an unshakable premonition lingered, a persistent instinct tugging at her. Perhaps it was the chaos she'd previously experienced when arriving at the Delhi airport and now she was about to face it again.

Trying to shrug it off and avoid dwelling on it, she grabbed her backpack and set off for the airport. Still a newbie at navigating the hectic atmosphere of international airports, she encountered passenger lines endlessly looping around as anxious travelers awaited their turn. Brenée, trying to figure out her place, peeked at the overhead monitors flickering with unceasing updates of arrivals and departures of airline companies she had never heard of before.

"Where do I need to go?" she asked herself while glancing at the booking reservation on her phone. "Turkish Airlines" was the first line she read at the top of the email reservation.

After locating the airline sign at the check-in counter, she rushed to get in line. The line was long with 30-35 people in front. Brenée looked at the clock and saw she had two hours before departure time.

Ok, I'm good, she thought as she continued waiting in line, taking deep breaths to steady her uneasiness.

After 50 minutes in line, she realized the only thing that was moving fast was time. The line advanced at a slow pace and Brenée felt that nervous feeling intensify again. With about five families still in front, her shoulder grew tenser with each passing minute, and she let out a grunt.

Ugh, I knew I should've arrived earlier! she thought.

Then finally, it was her turn. She saw the airline agent waive her hand and Brenée hurried towards her.

"Hello, I am flying to Barcelona. Here's my passport."

"To Barcelona, you said?" asked the ticketing agent.

"Yes, ma'am," Brenée answered.

"We don't have a flight to Spain today. Those flights are operated by IndiGo. May I see your reservation?" she asked. Brenée opened her phone to show the booking information and handed the phone over.

"You see this?" The agent pointed to the small print below the time. "This reads operated by IndiGo."

"Wait, but do you see this?" Brenée countered. "It shows Turkish Airlines at the top."

"Yes, it is Turkish Airlines, but operated by IndiGo. You need to go to their counter," the lady explained. With a wide-eyed gasp, Brenée grabbed her passport as she felt a wave of panic.

Looking for signs that would provide orientation, she found an information employee and asked for directions.

"Straight ahead," he pointed.

Brenée ran, her backpack bouncing with each stride only 55 minutes before departure. Once at the counter, she went to one of the agents ignoring the long lines.

"Hi, I was in line with Turkish Airlines for the past 65 minutes. I am going to Barcelona, and I waited in the wrong line. Can I still catch the flight?" Brenée asked, her voice edged with clear worry.

"The flight is closed. You need to go over there and talk to a customer service representative," the agent said, pointing to a module across the aisle.

Brenée practically cursed under her breath as she hurried to talk to someone who could help.

"Hello, I stood in line for over an hour at the wrong airline and now my flight to Barcelona is closed. Can you help me? I don't have any bags to check in," Brenée said, attempting to strengthen her plea.

The agent looked at Brenée, then the clock, and without saying a word, started typing on her keyboard.

The woman picked up the phone and made a call. Brenée listened to it intently, even when she didn't understand a word. She looked serene and calm, giving Brenée some hope. She continued typing a little more and hung up the phone.

"The flight is closed, but you are in. You have to hurry up as you still need to go through security. You got lucky because you have no bags to check in," the agent said as she handed the printed boarding passes to Brenée.

"Thank you! Thank you!" Brenée said, letting out a deep sigh and wiping her sweaty palms. And without wasting a moment, she rushed to the security line.

Finally airborne moving west towards Barcelona, she was set to fly 4,100+ miles, with an estimated travel time of 25 hours to include a lengthy 16-hour layover. "*16 hours?*" She noticed with a calm mind as she sat in her window seat. Brenée, curious, looked into her extended layover wanting to know what was waiting ahead.

"IST? Where is that?" she wondered. Connecting to in-flight internet, she was astonished to find out IST was the abbreviation for Istanbul, Turkey. "Wait, I'm going where?"

Without delay, Brenée continued checking the web to learn more about Istanbul, a place that deviated from her mom's script. Searching it up, she was pleasantly surprised to discover that the airline covered hotel room expenses for passengers with layovers exceeding eight hours.

"No way! A free hotel stay in Turkey?"

With a vibrant sunset unfolding above the clouds, Brenée crafted a short itinerary – this time an experience of her own creation.

I got it! She thought looking at her list. *My first stop will be the Blue Mosque!*

It was 10:07 at night when Brenée landed in Turkey. As one of the largest airports in the world, Brenée soon discovered the Istanbul airport resembled a modern indoor city, featuring endless passageways styled with a stunning blend of traditional Turkish elements and contemporary architecture. In this fusion of old and new, however, the language remained traditional as most airport employees spoke only Turkish. With that, Brenée was about to encounter the language barrier one more time.

"Excuse me, sir," she asked an employee walking by who seemed to be in a rush. "Can you tell me where customer service for Turkish Airlines is?" Without saying anything, the employee waved his armed signaling for Brenée to continue walking. Brenée, with a spark of optimism, kept walking, paying attention to the airport signs.

After minutes walking with no direction, she finally came upon a Turkish Airlines Customer Service desk.

"Hello, I have an overnight layover and need a room to stay tonight. Is that something you can help me with?" she asked in a friendly tone. The agent pointed to her boarding pass and passport while typing on his computer.

"Go downstairs to Customer Service. They will take you to the hotel," the agent said, his voice stiff and unfriendly.

"Sonraki kişi!" he called the next person, signaling Brenée to step aside.

Unsure of where "downstairs" was in the vastness of the airport, she began walking again aimlessly in search of a way down. She came across a group of people heading toward immigration and decided to follow.

Approaching the immigration officer, she handed over her passport. "Where is your visa?" the stern agent asked looking through the pages of her passport.

With a now nervous voice, Brenée replied, "I am not staying in Turkey, sir. I have an extended layover and fly out tomorrow."

"You need to get a visa if you want to leave the airport," the agent replied, tossing the passport back to Brenée.

Brenée took her passport with a sense of uneasiness settling over her body again, yet she took a deep breathe to steady herself.

"Okay, where do I go for that?" she asked, needing some direction.

"Go back!" the agent pointed his finger gesturing Brenée to get out of the line.

She turned back, *so much for a free hotel room! I am so tired and don't even know where I am sleeping tonight. I guess I'm sleeping on the floor.* She thought.

Crushed under the weight of her defeat and tired of chasing after the wind, she started to look for a place on the ground, tempted to retreat into her familiar hopeless pose.

From the depths of her self-pity, the old homeless man from Rishikesh came to mind. Seeing the obstacle, she realized she had options – stay stuck or leap forward.

Wait a second - I have been here before, mom. I recognize this moment, this challenge, and the obstacle ahead. This isn't new to me! I just lost sight of my Northern star. Now, let's look for the visa sign. It really can't be far! she thought, drawing optimism from her heart.

With a maze of endless corridors, Brenée saw signs in Turkish in every direction, none of them saying what she needed. She stopped at a directory screen but found nothing. Frustration bubbled up as time was slipping by.

Around the corner, finally - spotting "Visa" in the distance, Brenée saw light at the end of the dark tunnel. Rushing towards it, she took notice of the display through the customer window, "USA – $60," she read. Hope giving her courage again, she strode up to the young employee attending the visa counter.

"Hi, I fly out of Turkey tomorrow at 2 P.M. This is just a layover; do I still need to pay $60 dollars to enter the country for a few hours. I am spending less than a day here in Turkey," Brenée asked, showing her boarding pass through the glass. The agent pointed to the sign on the window saying something in Turkish.

"Yes, I understand, but you see, Turkey is not my final destination. I just have a long layover." The woman pointed again to the sign.

"Alright, alright. You know what? It doesn't matter, I just want to rest," Brenée said, evaluating her priorities and paying the fee.

Finally, out of immigration and officially downstairs, Brenée stepped into a fresh set of obstacles to figure out.

"Excuse me, can you tell me where Customer Service for Turkish Airlines is?" The employee shook his head no and continued walking. With determination as heavy as her backpack on her shoulders, Brenée kept wandering the long passages looking for more signs. There was no denying she was lost, but she kept pushing forward.

"Turkish Airlines you said?" asked an employee who strangely seemed willing to help. "Continue walking on this terminal for half a kilometer and you will find Customer Service to your left," the airport employee said.

"Thank you very much for your help!" Brenée replied, feeling a deep sense of relief. By now, midnight was creeping in, and she still didn't have a place to stay.

Walking for seven minutes, there was a spark of cheerfulness, "Could that be it?" she whispered.

Feeling like she had found the treasure with no map, she confirmed her details with the agent, who told her to wait for the shuttle to the hotel.

"Thank goodness, mom! I thought I'd end up sleeping on the airport floor tonight," she felt the weight of her stress lift off her shoulders.

With her mother's journal in her hands and finding a seat to catch a break, she entered a note she had floating in her head.

What was that nervous feeling I had right since I woke up in Delhi? Was that my intuition, almost a whisper of the future? Brenée wrote with her black pen as a gentle reflection so she wouldn't forget, *it was as if part of me sensed the struggles ahead. Wasn't that beyond strange?*

Right before closing the page, the shuttle driver yelled "Brenée," he said.

"Here, here!" Brenée raised her hand as she hurried to pack her mom's journal.

And with that, she was about to start an unexpected trip, off her mom's script.

March 29th:
Where East Kisses West

In the early morning stillness, as the clock barely approached 5 A.M., Brenée was abruptly awakened from a deep sleep. A loud, haunting chant seemed to be coming from her window, resonating from outside. The chanting sounded like a symphony of ethereal echoes that reached every corner of the ancient city. Voices rich with devotion carried out a singing conversation that Brenée could follow from beginning to end.

She lay in bed completely immobile with her body paralyzed by confusion and her face partially covered in blankets. Her heart pounded heavily. After five minutes of the swelling chant, complete silence descended. She waited a little longer. Still…silent.

"What the heck was that? It appears to be over," Brenée questioned reaching for her phone to search what on Earth had just happened. Not familiar with the deep-rooted cultural and religious customs, she found out it was *Adhan*, the first call to prayer of the day, a spiritual alarm clock that guided the city into a new day.

"Well, that was literally a spiritual awakening!" she exclaimed, laughing at her own silliness.

Jolted awake by the sudden chant, she gave up on sleep, deciding to get up and start her brief visit to Turkey.

Heading downstairs, she set out to enjoy her first Turkish meal, which consisted of a variety of foods she never thought she'd ever eat for breakfast – an array of cheeses, each with its own rich flavors, nuts offering an earthy crunch, and figs delicately drizzled with pure, golden sweetness. The waitress, a lady in her later years, covered her hair and neck with a black turban exposing only her face. Submissively pouring Brenée a cup of Turkish coffee, she avoided eye contact. Brenée, offering a friendly smile, thanked the lady with a bow just like in India. The lady smiled back, making brief eye contact.

Impatient for her very first taste of Turkish coffee, Brenée reached for a sip of the boldest brew looking as dark as midnight. With the strength of ten espressos extracted all in one, the black liquid hit her taste buds with a hard punch like two fighters in the crunch. *"hoa, that's a new level of coffee!* Brenée thought, feeling its rich, bold, and syrupy body. "This is too strong for my taste," she said to herself as the flavors slowly sank in, "but I wonder what mom would say about black Turkish coffee".

Placing the cup back on the table, she took note of how deeply she missed coffee from back home. And finishing her first Turkish meal, Brenée had six hours to explore.

"To the Blue Mosque, please," Brenée pointed to a picture on her phone to let the cab driver know where she wanted to go. The driver set off along the coast, while Brenée gazed out the back seat window, admiring the timeless city.

It was a journey into the past with every kilometer passing by. On the shore, seagulls took flight with their open wings in an everlasting dance silhouetting against the brightening sky. Further into the distance, Brenée spotted a long bridge crossing the ocean.

Amazing! That must be the Bosphorus Bridge that connects Europe with Asia, she thought, recalling her reads on the city.

After a few more minutes of driving, she was dropped off at the Blue Mosque, an impressive building beautifully decorated with blue ceramic titles of intricate design and exceptional craftsmanship. With a striking center dome edged by six slender towers, she saw loudspeakers mounted around them concluding that was the origin of the amplified echoing alarm clock that woke her up earlier in the day. Unable to go inside at that early hour of the morning, she decided to take a walk through the old streets and alleys speaking ageless stories of kings and warriors.

It was as if in Istanbul, every corner had a tale to tell.

As she rounded another corner, an unexpected breeze carrying the scent of the ocean washed over her face. Brenée realized she'd once again come face-to-face with the water. Captivated by the view and drawn to the mellow waves, she hurried across the street toward the rocky shoreline.

Sitting on a large rock, Brenée contemplated the vastness of the ocean stretching before her with a view of the Bosphorus Bridge in the distance. Spanning about 5,100 feet, the bridge was the kissing point between the two large continents.

"Mom, I can't believe I'm seeing this with my own eyes. It's like the pages of a book coming to life telling stories of the place where the East meets the West," she said out loud, her voice drifting on the sea breeze. Once again, she felt connected with her mother's magic, feeling her spirit wrap around her as a guardian angel. "I know I'm stepping away from your original plans, but I am so glad of this unexpected adventure."

Called to capture the feeling forever in her mind, Brenée closed her eyes and took a deep breath, a new skill she learned while in India. Savoring the moment of being present in this ancient land, she took a deep inhale, breathing in centuries of history lingering in the air and then breathing out a long exhalation as an offering of gratitude from the depths of her heart. Brenée repeated this several times, touching a world beyond her senses.

Here, in this place, she felt a deep sense of peace washing over her.

Still having a couple of hours to spare, she continued exploring the area, texting her dad and sending pictures of her unexpected trip. She stopped at a small, quaint restaurant where she had another little bite of Turkey – a golden cloud of creamy smoothness, hummus, with swirls of glistening virgin olive oil scooped by pockets of tender pittas. Brenée topped off the meal with an iconic baklava, a sweet indulgence for the soul made of layers of honey, nuts, and sheer pastry.

As the time drew near to continue her journey to Barcelona, Brenée returned to the hotel to collect her belongings and catch the shuttle back to the airport. It'd only been a brief stopover, yet she felt enlivened from her spontaneous adventure.

Now, it was time to keep heading west, crossing the Mediterranean from Turkey to Spain.

March 30th:
The Journey of a Million Steps

The morning sounds of traffic, voices and neighbors' ring tones going off could easily be heard through the thin walls of Brenée's short-term room rental. After a long day of travel the day before, Brenée was feeling jetlagged and wanted to wake up slowly to ease herself into the flow of the day. She rolled over to the other side of the bed to reach for her bag and grab her mother's journal to read.

"Okay, mom, I am in Spain. What do I do next?" she asked as she opened the journal on the next page.

Welcome to Barcelona, my Sunshine!

You are about to experience a culture with unparalleled friendliness, great music, and amazing food. After having savored the spices of India, you're bound to delight in the rich flavors of Spain.

Spain captivated my heart from the moment I arrived, every single time, all the time. There is so much to do that no visit ever offered the same experience. Of course, you may want to explore Barcelona and do the things tourists do, but then get ready for a hike.

A hike? What do you mean, Mom? Brenée, who had no particular hiking interests or skills, was unsure of what her mom could have been planning. She kept reading.

El Camino de Santiago is a popular pilgrimage route that has been traveled along since the Middle Ages. The story goes that the remains of Saint James, one of the 12 apostles of Jesus, is buried in the Cathedral of Santiago de Compostela, the final destination. There are several "caminos" or ways to get to Santiago, but you are to take El Camino Francés, the French way. That is ultimately the reason why you are in Barcelona.

When you are ready, take the train to Pamplona to join the pilgrimage that will cross the northern part of Spain by foot.

You will be hiking for a month or so, depending on the number of miles you are able to walk every day. You will find places to eat, shower, and sleep along your journey.

Once you get to Pamplona, come and see me again.

Happy travels!

~Mom

Brenée was speechless and did not know what to think.

"So, you want me to walk for how many days, you said?!" she went back to verify, "Mom! You know I'm not physically ready for this," she said with a touch of frustration.

After reading the big task that was about to follow, Brenée was so overwhelmed by it that all she did was to roll back into bed and go to sleep. "I'll deal with this later," she said.

Weaving around the thought of her next mission, Brenée decided to enjoy the bohemian vibes and surreal artistic expressions of Barcelona first.

She visited La Basilica de La Sagrada Familia, took a stroll through Las Ramblas to eat delicious tapas, and spent a serene afternoon watching a Spanish Sunset at Park Güell. Breathing in the magic of Gaudí's work, she witnessed how nature and architecture twirled in the artist's creative world.

After five sunsets in the city, the inevitable could no longer be put off. She set out for Pamplona - a town known for the daring men and women who run with the bulls every year at the Festival de San Fermin.

Brenée wasn't going there to run, but rather to walk a journey of a million steps.

To get to Pamplona, Brenée booked a ticket on their high-speed train cleverly called AVE (Alta Velocidad Española), which also means bird in Spanish. Faced pinned to the window, she watched 196 miles fly by in a short 2-hour ride.

Once in Pamplona, she was instantly immersed in the remarkable Gothic and Baroque architectural style that characterized the small town. Churches with big, pointed arches and soaring buttresses combined with the exquisitely elaborate stained glass windows.

Later that afternoon, on the cozy balcony of her room, Brenée sat on an old wooden bench overlooking the plaza below filled with colorful flowers in bloom.

With such beautiful view, she opened her mom's journal and read what she had to say to prepare for the walk ahead.

Hello, my Sunshine!

As you are preparing to start El Camino, know how excited I am for you! Walking El Camino is an incredible journey – not just across miles, but within yourself. Every step you take takes you closer to a destination of empowerment, self-awareness, and mental strength.

Here's a few things to keep in mind:

I recommend you carry what you need – the less you carry, the further you'll go.

Trust the path, even when it's unclear - there will be days of doubt and sore feet but keep going. The path will rise to support you for as long as you keep walking.

Embrace the silence - there will be stretches with no Wi-Fi or distractions. Use that silence. It is not empty – it is full of insights.

Every blister will have a lesson - listen to what it's teaching you and adjust what needs to be changed.

Embrace the art of slowing down - sometimes you will walk many miles, other times, you will walk none. It is okay to take a break and recharge.

Be patient - you don't walk 500 miles in one day. What is required of you is simple - take one step at a time for as long as you can in a day.

And lastly, believe in your determination - you don't have to be fearless, you just must be determined.

Remember that New Year's celebration when we were searching for a "word of the year" to capture our intentions? We both came up with the same word at the same time. Remember that?

Determination is our word, Brenée. Determination.

Once you get to Santiago de Compostela, come and see me again.

This is the way, Brenée. Walk in it.

Buen camino!

~Mom

Yes, I remember, mom, Brenée recalled tenderly as the memory traversed inside. *It was as if we were reading each other's minds.*

Determination! Tomorrow, I start a month-long pilgrimage - the journey of a million steps - with determination.

April 6th:
Footsteps of a Young Pilgrim

The air was crisp, carrying a subtle scent of dew-laden grass. A towering cathedral in the small-town square reminded Brenée it was 8:00 A.M.

As the morning rays of sunshine painted Pamplona with warm hues of orange, Brenée stood ready – ready to follow the footsteps of the sun. She paused for a moment before the iconic scallop shell marker on a cobblestone street, her heart quietly announcing that she stood at the beginning of the pilgrimage path.

In her backpack, snugly strapped to her shoulders, were the essentials for the month ahead on El Camino de Santiago –carefully chosen items like an easily accessible map, her pilgrim's passport, and a walking stick – for whatever the road might bring. Of course, her mother's ashes were safely packed in an inside pocket.

Brenée felt uncertainty coursing through her veins, yet she also felt a hint of excitement lingering beneath the surface. The thought of traveling on foot, with no set plans and only the hope of finding a place to stay each night, was both thrilling and intimidating – like setting sail without a chart, letting the wind and stars determine where she'd land. To reassure herself, Brenée promised her dad to text him at the end of each day to feel safe.

"Well, here I come, mom!" she whispered as the young pilgrim took her first step, imprinting her footstep on the gravel beneath her shoe. Little did she know, the crunching sound of her prints would eventually become the soundtrack of her pilgrimage. The sacred journey had begun, and with each stride, Brenée left her fingerprints, embracing the determination her mom had described.

As she walked through centuries-old streets in picturesque villages, breath-taking fields, and rolling hills, her enthusiasm mingled with the serenity of the path. Vibrant wildflowers moved to the rhythm of the summer breeze, and the distant sound of a church bell marked the passing of time by announcing it was now 10:00 A.M.

It was easy to find beauty in all things, inviting Brenée to complete five more miles on her first day of pilgrimage. She started with a clear vision and plan, determined to end the day on a high note.

Even though she was walking alone, she definitely didn't feel lonely.

"Buenos dias, peregrina! Buen camino!" (Good morning, pilgrim! Good journey!) was the greeting from several fellow pilgrims, some strangers and others soon-to-be friends, as they exchanged smiles and nods.

"Gracias, igualmente!" (Thank you, likewise!) Brenée found herself responding back to the many pilgrims walking in front of her, eventually behind and alongside her too.

People from literally many walks of life were united by El Camino.

With each passing mile, her uneasiness about walking El Camino gradually transformed into pure excitement, a feeling that became her companion and carried her forward one step at a time. This feeling gave way to the realization that El Camino de Santiago was not just a physical journey but a profound peregrination of discovery with the self and the world around her.

As the sun continued to ascend, Brenée enjoyed the random cloud shade on the scorching sunny day. Even under the warm glow over the landscape, she embraced the path, eager to unravel the stories hidden within each cobblestone, each medieval castle, and each old church. It was only day one on the path and with every step, she could already sense a closer and deeper feeling into the heart of El Camino.

The road offered so much enjoyment that Brenée took only quick breaks to eat, use the restroom, and change her sweaty socks.

It was then, when the clock ticked past 4:50 P.M after eight hours of walking, that Brenée realized she indeed had covered her daily goal of 12 miles. She knew the sunset would soon arrive, and a deeper urgency drove her to push toward the nearest town to find a roof for the night.

On weary feet, Brenée arrived at a charming village named Puente la Reina (Bridge of the Queen), taking its name from the historic medieval bridge that stood nearby.

She saw a group of pilgrims flocking into an albergue (a pilgrim hostel) and decided to follow their lead.

"Buenas noches, peregrina," she was greeted with a lisp in the lips by a Spanish man at the front desk. "Buenas noches," Brenée replied. "I need a place to stay tonight; do you have a bed for me?"

"Vale! (sure), We do. Let me have your El Camino passport to stamp it," the man asked.

"Oh si, I have it in here somewhere," Brenée said, trying to reach inside her stuffed backpack. After opening all the pockets in her bag, Brenée exclaimed, "Oh, here it is!"

"You may want to keep this handy. You will get it stamped along the way to track and record your walk," the man advised as he stamped her passport in a firm and deliberate motion. Brenée agreed and proceeded to pay the small fee, while the man started walking Brenée towards her bunk bed.

She had never seen a place like this before. It was like a combination of hotel and shelter with dozens of bunk beds in one big open space. "The showers and restrooms are that way," he pointed to the left corner of the large room. "And the cafeteria is that way," he pointed to the opposite corner.

"Thank you. Really what I want first is a shower!" Brenée said.

"I am sure," the man replied with a knowing smirk on his face.

Brenée could hardly believe she'd done it. She'd completed 12 miles and her first sleep arrangements upon arrival. As she headed to the shower, she couldn't help but to spread a big smile across her face.

"I did well today, mom," she said.

"Good morning, señorita! Ready for another day?" an older woman asked while tying up her shoes from the bunk bed across Brenée's.

"Good morning," Brenée replied while placing a band aid on her foot. "Yes! Once I take care of this blister," followed by a big ouch.

The lady smiled. "You know, I recommend using mole skin instead of band aids. It reduces friction. Runner's trick of the trade!" she said as she handed over a couple pieces.

"What is the difference?" Brenée asked, turning them over to see the back.

"These are thick and soft and if you cut a hole, it will provide cushion around your blister," her voice carried a motherly tone as she spoke.

"Oh, I see what you mean," Brenée listened as she peeled off the backing in a single pull.

"Is this your first time walking El Camino?" she asked wanting to engage a light conversation.

"It is. I'm really not a hiker, a runner or anything like that. In fact, I didn't even know this route existed until a few days ago," Brenée said with a chuckle.

"Wait, let me get this straight - you recently learned about El Camino and decided to sign up for a month-long hike? That's incredible! I've been planning this for years," She laughed making fun of the situation.

"Well, no. Not exactly," Brenée proceeded. "All this was mom's idea."

"Oh, great. What a coincidence! I am also here with my son. His name is Leo. He's getting ready now," the lady said. "So, where's your mom?" she asked wanting to know more.

"My mom…" Brenée paused, taking a moment not wanting her emotions to show. "…died last year and left instructions for me to spread her ashes at the end of El Camino," Brenée explained.

"Oh my God, I'm sorry I asked. I didn't mean to stir up sad emotions. I'm deeply sorry about your loss," the lady replied apologetically, reaching out to place a kind hand on Brenée's shoulder.

"No worries. It's okay. Last year was rough; I felt as if life was over for me, but I'm gradually figuring out how to deal with the sadness. I think finding my mom's instructions gave me a spark of purpose and hope. I feel good about carrying out her plans. To be honest, they felt pretty intimidating at first, but I've realized that each day away from home gets a little easier. I've seen a lot, experienced so much, and picked up some really valuable lessons along the way."

"This is truly exceptional. I'm touched by your story," the woman said. "As for me, I'm here with my son spending some quality time together as we bring our adventure list to life. We are from Vancouver. Where are you from?" she asked, intrigued.

"I am from Texas. El Paso, Texas," Brenée replied.

"Oh yes, I've passed through there!" the woman said.

"You have?" Brenée replied in surprise.

"Yes, we stopped there on our drive to the Copper Canyon in Mexico. It's only a few hours south of the border. I was young, wild, and free," she laughed, "a hippie, you would say. I joined some friends, and we drove all the way from Canada down to Mexico. Uff, it feels like it was a lifetime ago!" she said with another laugh. "You see, I was a runner and wanted to meet the natives from Chihuahua. They have been running for centuries – the Tara...wait, Tarahumaras," she said with difficulty.

"Oh yeah, of course! I've seen documentaries on them. I believe they run marathons in sandals. It's mind blowing," Brenée said with an added hand-explosion gesture.

"Exactly! It's amazing. I used to run only in tennis shoes!" Her laughter was rich, genuine, and warm, inviting Brenée to enjoy the conversation.

"You know? What a wild connection. My mom was a runner too. She lost her life in a pedestrian-car accident while out running," Brenée said, getting choked over the last words.

"That's awful!" the lady said changing her tone. "I can't even imagine how hard this has been for you and your family. People are so careless behind the wheel these days. They forget they're driving a machine that can kill. My son almost got hit by a public bus that ran a red light the other day. He was leaving campus and walking back to the dorms. He said the bus missed him by a hair! It's terrible, really."

"Nothing ever happened to me back in my running days and now, well, I don't run nearly as much as I used to. My knees get angry at me when I do!" big laugh, "Now, I mostly walk," She looked around their bustling hostel. "And speaking of walking, where is my son? It's time to start the day. Would you like to walk with us this morning? I'd love to hear more about your mom," she kindly said.

"I'd love to," Brenée responded with happiness warming her smile.

"Where are my manners? We've talked for a while, and I haven't introduced myself. I'm Emma and my son, who is finally back from the shower is Leo," she said as her son walked toward them.

"And I am Brenée," Brenée introduced herself.

"Sweetheart, I want you to meet Brenée. She will be walking with us today," Emma said.

"Hi, Brenée. Nice to meet you!" Leo said extending his arm for a handshake.

"Okay! Are we ready now? We need to get going," Emma looked at her watch.

"I have mole skin on and am good to go!" Brenée replied.

"Well, let's get going!" Emma enthusiastically ordered.

Heading out into the morning sunshine, the young pilgrim started her second day, no longer leaving solo prints of her footsteps, but now walking in stride with her new friends.

April 7th:
Band Of Seekers

The sun hung bright in the sky, casting a warm feeling on the skin. As Brenée walked side-by-side with the small group, she formed an instant friendship born out of shared stories and the common goal of crossing Spain on this ancient pilgrimage route. Conversation flowed easily about everything and anything, weaving tales with big laughter and shared reflections.

Miles away from home, Brenée learned about life in Vancouver while Emma and Leo learned about what it was like to live in the hot desert of the Southwest. Strangers moments ago, Brenée and her friends moved as a band of seekers, united by the collective curiosity and appreciation for the beauty unfolding around them. They advanced through the path as travelers, almost like explorers in search of the hidden treasure on the map.

Brenée and her band were not the only seekers on the road, though. They were drops of water in a sea of innumerable pilgrims they shared the path with. The variety of noises communally created- crunching gravel, jingling walking sticks, various languages from different corners of the globe – were some of the sounds that accompanied Brenée's steady progression.

On the path, she felt a symphony of emotions that expanded and extended, developing a profound sense of connection. This connection invited Brenée, the once-quiet young woman, to strike conversations with other pilgrims wanting to hear stories and anecdotes of their own reasons for walking this path of transformation.

Her footsteps synchronized into a delicate rhythm with the rest as the landscape shifted subtly from lush meadows to quaint villages with stone houses that seemed frozen in time. Friendly locals greeted Brenée and the group with smiles and encouragement, reinforcing the sense of a shared human connection that transcended all borders. In this place, there were no migrants. Everyone belonged.

Conversations certainly made the 14 miles covered that day feel like a breeze. At a rustic wayside inn in the town of Estella, Brenée and the group decided to stop and rest for the night.

That night for dinner, they put together a spontaneous picnic as they sat on weathered benches, sharing meals and swapping more stories. The simple pleasure of eating together deepened the bond and friendship they were forming.

For the next several days, Brenée, Emma and Leo resumed the journey together over and over again. Countless times, Brenée saw, in their interactions, reflections of her mother and herself.

With the journals in hand, Brenée felt the presence of her mother with them as well. Perhaps her mom's company felt more intense during the panoramic vision of the countryside as the sun dipped below the horizon, bathing the landscape in a magical sunset. Hard to say, however, if it was the most intense during the dark nights covered in stars emerging like distant lights in the vast sky. Either way, Brenée knew her mom was next to her.

After fifteen sunsets and 250 miles, Brenée and her two friends had reached the half-way point of their journey. As they approached the City of León, they found a humble yet comfortable albergue, which they agreed would be a good place to rest for an entire day.

Feeling physically exhausted, they decided to recharge in solitude in their own separate rooms.

With a whole day free to do as they wished, they ironically felt like doing nothing at all.

After a well-deserved day of relaxation, Brenée resumed her pilgrimage with Emma and Leo when the stroke of the church bell announced to the town it was 8 A.M. With a fresh outlook and refreshed energy, the three started walking towards Villar de Mazarife, thirteen miles from León. They were happy to think that their next full rest stop would be at her final destination, the town of Santiago de Compostela.

As they started the second half, they decided to be a bit more adventurous and wander off the path away from the highway. Escaping some of the crowds, the pilgrims took the alternative rural route, which provided more peaceful time of silence, connection, and introspection.

Under sunshine, rain or wind, for the next fourteen sunsets, Brenée, Emma, and Leo averaged fifteen miles each day. They supported and encouraged each other in the midst of blisters and cramps, sharing stories and silence alike.

A sense of excitement grew stronger with each glimpse of the signs announcing the shrinking distance to Santiago de Compostela.

Each step brought them closer and closer to their goal, and before Brenée knew it, thirty sunsets and 440 miles had passed.

With only sixteen more miles under the sun, it felt unreal the month-long journey was almost done.

May 7th:
Cracking Open the Cocoon

It was the last evening on the path, and the small band arrived to their final albergue in time to have dinner with a sunset coloring the western sky. As they chatted happily and gathered around a table draped in white, they heard a young male voice greeting them, "Buenas tardes, peregrinas," Brenée and the group turned their heads to find out it was a group of four who had caught up to them.

"Can we join you for dinner?" one of the guys asked.

"Definitely, of course," Brenée invited them, moving her chair to make room for their new friends.

"We just ordered food and plan to sit here without moving much for the next two hours. My old knees need a break," Emma said with a laugh.

"Oh, I know. My feet need rest too. I have blisters that turned into callus," someone else said.

"This one! This one was the worst!" Brenée said as she pointed to the back of her ankle where the shoe rubbed her skin.

"I tried band aids, double socks, and even toilet paper taped to my skin. The only thing that alleviated the problem was mole skin, old runner's trick!" she said smiling at Emma.

"It is! But you know what I think is the most amazing trick you learned, Brenée?" Emma asked, leaning in with a smile. "You faced every challenge - big and small - and somehow, you made it work. At first, you didn't think you could finish this month-long hike alone and now... look at how confident you are with the unknown. You are totally comfortable being uncomfortable. You opened yourself to explore the path unfolding before you and now you are only a few miles away from the finish line. I am sure your mom would be very proud of you."

"Your words mean a lot to me, but I need to say, though..." Brenée clarified, "I didn't do this alone. Your company kept me going even when I felt weary. Without you both, I probably would've given up halfway through. In your voice, I heard my mom's guidance several times. Thank you, Emma and Leo. Really," Brenée said with warmth radiating through her heart.

"You did the work," Leo said, "the drive was always in you – we were just lucky to watch it up close," Leo gave Brenée a soft shoulder rub with the compliment.

"Well, here's to crossing paths with strangers who then become a story worth telling." Brenée raised her wine glass, "Salud!"

"Cheers!" "Salute!" "Saúde!" different voices united to one to make the toast. As the night arrived, the feast continued with great glee, tales, and experiences of the trail. Some spoke of the breathtaking landscapes they had traversed, while others recounted the challenges they had overcome.

And it was in this intimate moment of laughter when the stars called Brenée by her name. Feeling herself awakening to life beneath the full moon, the butterfly had finally cracked open the cocoon. She recognized she had shed her layers of fear and was not the same shy, young girl anymore. Brenée was now an independent, brave, and strong woman, walking towards the end of the road.

May 8th:
A Balm for the Hurting Heart

U nder a blushing sunrise glow, Brenée woke up ready to walk the last 14 miles left to explore. Heading towards the assigned starting point, the Plaza in front of an ancient church, the bell announced she was early. Overhead, high above, Brenée observed the full moon still lingering with a fainted silvery haze, refusing to leave the morning sky and reminding her of the traces of the previous night.

Her muscles were sore giving her the idea to lay a towel on the lawn. She placed her hands and knees in table pose, circling her hips around in one direction, and then, in the opposite direction. Moving to the rhythm of her breath, she engaged her toes and lifted her hips high towards the sky in downward facing dog. Stepping into a forward fold, she then raised her arms up high, placing her palms together down to her heart.

At that moment, Brenée let her movements be a prayer to the soul feeling a deep sense of gratitude washing over her. She was thankful for her mother, who even after she was gone had guided her out of her comfort zone. She was grateful for the stories, experiences, and lessons learned. Lastly, she was appreciative for standing tall in tree pose, embracing her growth so far away from home.

Planting her bare feet like strong roots, she grew stable into the ground. At the same time, her arms stretched upward like branches blooming and reaching skyward. Brenée felt a hug from her mom with a gentle warmth radiating through her body from the tip of her fingers down to the tip of her toes.

Brenée smiled into the horizon and said, "I know you are proud of me, mom. I am too."

"Good morning, Brenée! Are you ready?" Emma asked interrupting Brenée in child's pose.

"Uh…hey! Good morning. I guess it's already 8 o'clock," Brenée replied looking at the time, "Sorry if we interrupted you. What was that you were doing? Looked kindda… peaceful," Leo asked curious. "Oh, yoga. I learned it in India," Brenée replied. "Yoga? Isn't that… stretching?" Emma asked. "Well…it's way more than that. It's a moving meditation, stretching your body and giving you feel-good vibes," Brenée explained. "Hmm, feel-good vibes, uh? Teach us!" Leo asked. "Let's do it!" Brenée guided Emma and Leo into their first yoga pose.

Following a short flow, it was time to take off to Santiago de Cospostela.

Tightly strapping their backpacks to their bodies and holding the trek sticks in their hands, Brenée and the soul circle walked at a moderate pace for the next five hours to their final destination. Committed to pushing all the way through until reaching La Plaza do Obradoiro in front of La Basilica de Santiago de Compostela, their feet were tired, their bodies fatigued, but in the inside, their hearts felt the feel-good vibes that stirred the air before the journey's end.

"Ta-da-da-DAAA! Alright, boys and girls! This may be the last yellow scallop sign we follow," Emma announced in a fanfare, pointing out to the iconic fan-like shape with lines radiating to one point that had been guiding them all throughout El Camino.

"Bienvenidos Peregrinos! (Welcome Pilgrims)," Brenée read the sign and translated for Emma and Leo.

"We are here!" the pilgrims cheered, jumping up and down in delight, embracing in a group hug.

Amid unparalleled excitement, Brenée said out loud, "Mom! I can't believe I did it! I walked across Spain for 31 sunsets on El Camino de Santiago!"

"I know your mom is celebrating with us right now! We are so proud of you, Brenée," Emma said.

"You both made the journey so much lighter. I will never forget this experience," Brenée got teary-eyed.

To properly seal the journey, Brenée and the small group linked arms and walked a few more feet to the heart of the town to La Plaza do Obradoiro. Once there, they went into La Catedral de Santiago de Compostela to give thanks for their successful journey and safe arrival to the end of their pilgrimage.

When they went in, they sat near the back as the sunlight streamed through the blend of dazzling colors of the church's stained-glass windows, casting a rainbow over the polished pews.

The air was heavy with the scent of burning candles, incense, and the sound of hushed whispers echoing through the sacred space.

Enveloped in a mixture of awe and disbelief, Brenée reached for her bag and grabbed her mom's journal to read.

Hello, my Sunshine!

If you are reading these lines, you have completed El Camino. What an accomplishment! Appreciate the importance of this experience as it is a transformative event. I am certain you turned strangers into good friends and casual conversations into meaningful life lessons. I am sure you met people from places you didn't even know existed and got to hear stories you thought only possible in dreams.

I know you got tired and almost wanted to quit, yet seeing other people continuing the path motivated you. I am certain at times you felt lost, while at others, you knew exactly where to go. I know this because that's simply how life goes.

El Camino is a summarized version of life itself where the only thing required is simple – that you put one foot in front of the other. Just keep on walking no matter how steep, hilly, or challenging it gets.

I know you have reached the end of El Camino, but our El Camino is not over yet. After you rest for some time in Santiago, take a bus to head to the village of Finisterre.

In the times of the Roman Empire, this was believed to be the edge of the world before America was discovered. Literally, the name Finisterre in Latin is Finis Terrae, end of the Earth. When you arrive in the village, walk to the remarkable lighthouse on the rocky cape during the sunset. Continue to the cliff and once there, let my ashes seal the journey of our El Camino.

Brenée, I will be delighted to know our walk together on the El Camino concluded at the very end of the world.

Happy travels!

~Mom

Brenée, after reading her mother's words, felt wrapped in melancholy. Her soul ached, from a pain that reached her very core. Mute tears spilled down her cheeks, as she put her mom's journal to the side. She knelt on the hassock and burst into inconsolable sobs. It was an overwhelming feeling of emotions rushing together all at once. The church itself seemed to cradle Brenée in an ancient embrace providing a sanctuary for her emotions.

Emma gently placed a comforting hand over her shoulder but didn't try to stop Brenée from crying. This was a soft reminder that Emma and Leo were there in silent support if she needed them.

In the serenity of the church, Brenée's emotions swirled like a storm as she felt the immense weight of her mother's physical absence. Her mother was gone. Truly gone. And in that moment, deep in her heart, she felt a hole.

When her body could cry no more, Brenée turned around, wiped her tears away and placed her hand on top of Emma's lap offering a timid smile. A sense of gratitude began to emerge, born from the realization that her new friends were there sharing her grief and giving her love that acted as a balm for her hurting heart.

After the storm, tranquility followed. The church, with its timeless structure and echoes of countless prayers, became the sanctuary she'd needed to drain her sorrows and find peace.

"I'm sorry; I just had a moment. Since I found my mom's journals shortly after her death, I became so absorbed by her plans that I didn't seal my pain and grief properly...until now," Brenée said.

"No need to apologize, Brenée. This is a very special and sublime moment for us as well. Look around you and notice the countless number of pilgrims who are finishing El Camino today. We all are here for a reason and maybe that reason is that deep down, we all have bruises in our hearts. Otherwise, why would we go through a month-long hike of reflection, escaping from the routine of our daily lives? We all, in some way and to some degree, came here to heal our wounds and restore some aspects of our lives one step at a time," Emma said, her eyes filling with tears of compassion.

"Come on. Let's go outside to get some fresh air. The air is too thick in here plus I don't want to be next feeling nostalgic," Emma said, trying to contain her tears.

Brenée nodded as they all stood to walk out of the sacred space, finding strength in their collective embrace.

Brenée hadn't quite realized that in celebrating the end of her pilgrimage, she was also reaching the end of her time traveling with Emma and Leo. She enjoyed their last time together grabbing lunch, as they rested their fatigued bodies.

"So where are you going next, Brenée?" Leo asked with curiosity.

"Well, I take the bus to the village of Finisterre tomorrow afternoon. From there, I'll take a train to Madrid and once there, I'll find out where mom wants me to go next," Brenée explained.

"Keep in touch on social media. Please post pictures of wherever you end up next," Leo asked Brenée as they hugged.

"I will for sure, Leo," Brenée reassured the young man. "And you, Emma…" Brenée paused as she reached for her hand. "Thank you for taking care of me during this journey. There were several times that I was able to hear my mom speak through you. Thank you for your motherly love and for reminding me of what that feels like." Emma pulled Brenée into a warm hug, eyes shimmering with tears.

"You are a very special girl, Brenée. Never forget that. On a path with a thousand pilgrims, I'm so glad our destinies merged. If you ever need guidance or simply a listening ear, I am here for you. We are family now," Emma said.

"I sure will, Emma," Brenée agreed as they began to part ways.

"Goodbye, Emma and Leo. What an amazing experience we shared together," Brenée said, "I came to Spain alone and I leave with the best soul mates I've ever known."

"Safe travels, Brenée! We will be in touch and plan another great adventure in the near future – until we meet again!" Emma and Leo waived goodbye.

Leaving the two behind, Brenée concluded her month-long pilgrimage for her mom, herself, and the woman she had become.

May 9th:
At The Edge of The World

The charter bus rumbled in the afternoon light of Santiago de Compostela, as Brenée settled into a window seat. The worn, comfortable upholstery paired with soft music in her headphones cradled her while the bus began its journey towards the mystical coastal town of Finisterre.

From Santiago de Compostela to Finisterre, it was only a two-hour drive through the picturesque scenery of rolling prairies, charming villages, and lush greenery that stretched mile after mile. Brenée, oblivious to the now-familiar scenery, spent the sixty-mile journey wrapped in her inner contemplation of the pilgrimage she'd just completed.

Wanting to capture the moment, she found an empty space in her mom's journal. With her black pen she wrote, "I completed El Camino de Santiago after a month-long hike. I am now on my way to Finisterre." Marking her sentence with a date, she went back to her inner reflections as she gazed out the window.

The bus let out a low hiss as the air brakes engaged, followed by the deep hum of the engine winding down, before coming to a complete halt.

"Hemos llegado a la Villa de Finisterre (We have arrived at the Village of Finisterre)," Brenée's thoughts were sharply interrupted by the announcement from the driver.

"What? We're here already?" Brenée felt as though she had just sat down.

Back on the move once more, Brenée disembarked and stepped onto the cobbled pavement to be immediately welcomed by the ancient port surrounded by waters from the Atlantic Ocean.

Finisterre was a small village, perhaps inconsequential in size. Poetic legends, however, said that at Cape Finisterre, people could find the earth's most majestic sunsets. And Brenée was there to do just that.

Not far out in the distance, Brenée spotted the rocky cape with its remarkable lighthouse – the lighthouse that her mom described in her journal. Walking towards the coastline of rocky shores, Brenée leaned forward on the rock wall to see she was standing on a colossal cliff. From her vantage point, she saw a trail down below that led to the lighthouse. In that moment, Brenée felt drawn to explore this place of ancient legends with an intuitive need.

"Listen to your gut," Brenée remembered her mother's words and decided to follow through to discover where the path led. As she walked the narrow dirt trail, the waters seemed to create a theatrical drama – the waves danced with beauty and grace as they crashed against the rugged coastline.

Then, Brenée decided to deviate from the path to balance on the boulders alongside the trail, where the land ended and the sea began. With the vast ocean stretching before her, Brenée rose tall and brave, her posture strong and unwavering. Reaching inside her backpack for her mom's ashes, Brenée gently removed the container top and raised it high up in the sky with one hand.

"Mom, we have arrived at the end of the world!" Brenée declared victoriously across the waves. "And now, right here, right now, our El Camino is sealed."

With warmth filling her heart and the wind whipping the tears from her eyes, she waived the container to spread her mom's ashes out in the air to be carried down onto the ocean.

Like a lady on the hill, she remained standing on the rocks, marveling at the beauty of the sunset as the sun slowly hid behind the ocean. Brenée had in fact found the perfect sunset whispered in poems and imagined in dreams.

She found it standing tall, holding her mother's ashes at the edge of the world.

May 12th:
European Charm in an Espresso Cup

Over the course of the next few days, Brenée made her way from Finisterre down to the heart of Spain. With her family in the coffee business, she was always open to explore Cafés at each new place.

In Madrid, she became an avid fan of "café con leche" (coffee with milk) at a specialty coffee shop tucked away within the narrow alleys of the city. Brenée, with her selective taste, promptly considered Ambu a true space of brewing art.

At the start of her mornings, she'd visit the cozy Café embraced by old world European charm infused by the sounds of espresso dripping into a cup. "Whoosh!, Hisss!" the familiar buzz of steam followed the soft knocking of baristas tamping coffee grounds was the morning melody Brenée wanted to hear.

Sitting at a rustic wooden table with Madrid displayed at the window, Brenée wrapped her index finger through the handle of the small cup as its aromas wafted like soft words in the air. She glanced down and paused, captivated. The surface of her café con leche exquisitely adorned with a cloud of milk intricately forming a rosetta that delighted her senses. With each sip, Brenée felt the silky foam and rich espresso dance together in her mouth. In the midst of this caffeinated affair, Brenée snapped a picture of her cup and sent it to her dad, "Thinking of you dad," she texted. "Enjoying an out-of-this-world café con leche. Love you!"

And after hitting Send, Brenée reached for her mom's journal to find out where she'd be going next.

Hello, my Sunshine!

As you leave this beautiful country and prepare for the next leg of our adventure, know that our early lineage came from Spain. Legend says that many generations ago, my family traced its roots to Spain carrying a rich Muslim heritage. History agrees with the stories my father used to tell, revealing that Muslim armies came from the northern part of Africa and crossed into the Iberian Peninsula to conquer this country.

Then, as you know, Spain eventually discovered Las Americas and conquered its natives. This demonstrates that all humans are the product of thousands of years of countless connections in this tapestry woven by the forces of history.

I am happy to leave part of my ashes in Finisterre – where my early roots come from – and now it's time to make my final journey to the place of my indigenous ancestors, Mexico.

In Mexico, you are going to Oaxaca, a place I once visited years ago. While there, I invite you to find the similarities of India and Mexico in their colorful culture, flavorful dishes, and detailed artistry. I found it mind-blowing to experience how two places, worlds apart, could be so similar in so many ways.

Oaxaca, as you will see, will bring color to your soul. I promise.

Love you,

~Mom

Raising her cup to her lips for the last sip, with the café con leche now colder than before, Brenée closed her mother's journal and felt a silent roar.

After forty sunsets beneath the Spanish sky, it was time to fly 5,600 miles across the Atlantic Ocean. The final part of her epic mission was waiting in Oaxaca, the land of dark sauce and artistic devotion.

May 15th:
The Spirit of Color

Brenée got her face up against the airplane window and watched Madrid expose its urban beauty one last time. A golden glow gradually bathed the city, and traffic started to form an endless, fast-moving web of lights. It's said a mystic perceives the whole rather than parts – and in seeing the whole, they naturally understand where each part belongs.

That evening, as the plane ascended, Brenée could have very well been described as a mystic as she could see the lights of traffic resemble a web of countless neuro dots.

I agree with you, Mom. Everything in this world is indeed connected, Brenée thought. *We are cells that spark the soul. From this angle, I can see no separation. We come together to form the whole.*

Brenée checked into her room at a place defined as a Bed & Bread (cleverly described after the artisanal bakery nestled right next door). The bakery filled the B&B air with delightful, mouthwatering aromas like the smell of freshly baked cakes, buttery pastries, and warm bread, making Brenée's stomach growl. Her exhaustion was stronger than her hunger, though, inviting Brenée to relax and dine in.

Per the host's recommendation, she climbed two easy flights of stairs to the charming rooftop terrace to wait for her food. It was a lovely space decorated with black pottery, lush plants, and earthy tones. Settling in at a rustic table with dim lanterns hanging overhead, Brenée felt completely absorbed by the stunning colorful views of the city that surrounded her.

Much like in India, the vibrant spirit of color was woven into every corner of Oaxaca– houses painted in fuchsia, blue, and purple, while the streets were decorated with multicolor papel picado (Mexican party banners) in celebration of absolutely no particular occasion. This was also a town deeply rooted in religion. Brenée counted not one, not two, not three, but seven church towers with bells ringing in the distance announcing she was in a faithful town.

"Señorita, una copita de Mezcal cortesía de la casa (a Mezcal shot on the house)," the host, a man with a salt-and-pepper beard, approached her with a friendly smile, interrupting Brenée's observations.

"Oh gracias! Nunca he probado Mezcal (I have never had Mezcal before)," she thanked him for the gesture with both curiosity and apprehension.

"It is a handcrafted Mezcal from a local distillery in the mountains. When in Oaxaca, you must try Mezcal," he replied proudly. Brenée picked up the copita to perceive the amber liquid shimmer with a warm glow as she felt the cup's delicate craftsmanship in her hands. She was guided to swirl the Mezcal, releasing its complex aromas. The smoky essence of roasted agave filled her senses, intermingled with hints of earth and spice. She took a tentative sip, savoring the intricate display of flavors that unfolded on her palate.

"Oh wow, this is quite unique!" she said, after her first sip. The warmth of the Mezcal spread through her body, bringing a sense of appreciation for the ancient traditions of the region. Surprised by how much she enjoyed it, Brenée took another sip, embracing the liquid spirit of Oaxaca in its Mezcal.

"I will take my time drinking this copita. Gracias," she said.

As she resumed savoring the evening, she pulled out her mother's journal and penned a thought that night, "In Oaxaca now. I tried Mezcal and it seems like something you would love, mom. I think I might love it too!"

After dinner and back in her room, Brenée found a few flyers on a wooden stand strategically advertising local businesses and tours. One flyer in particular caught Brenée's attention, making her take a second look.

"Oaxacan Journey – Explore Oaxaca like Never Before! Day trip to Hierve El Agua and Arbol de Tule. Tours Wednesdays, Fridays and Saturdays starting promptly at 7 A.M. For reservations, call or text us through WhatsApp," she read it out loud as if talking to her mom.

With spontaneous energy, she was moved to make reservations for the following day. In less than five minutes, Brenée went from no plans to a day-long schedule leading the way.

There you have it mom, Brenée thought feeling a tingle of pride, *I'm officially an expert at spontaneous planning*, laughing at herself.

Brenée grabbed her tote bag, where she packed her hat, sandals, and sunscreen. She mapped the walking distance to the tour meeting point at Barrio de San Matias Jalatlaco, an area known for its artistic murals, cobblestone streets, and adobe homes.

Arriving at the meeting point, she noticed a white van with a young couple standing next to it.

That must be my tour, she thought, approaching the guides.

"Hola! Mi nombre es Brenée. Es éste el tour de Hierve El Agua? (Is this the tour for Hierve El Agua?)" she asked.

"Buenos dias, si! Brenée, verdad? Estabamos esperandote. Mi nombre es Roberto y ella es Lupita (Brenée, right? We were waiting for you. My name is Roberto and this is Lupita). We are expecting two more people, but feel free to find a seat in the van and wait inside. The A/C is running," he said.

"Perfecto!" she replied.

Once in the van, Brenée started picking up on different spoken accents; a young couple speaking with the traditional intonation and rhythm of the "Chilango" style from Mexico City, another couple with a quick and punchy delivery from New York City, and a mother and daughter with the classic and distinctive tone from Australia.

"Hola amigos! Thank you for joining us. A few quick announcements, so do listen up!" Roberto, the guide, interrupted the conversations in this big melting pot as two more people hopped on and found a seat.

"The group is now complete, and we are ready to start our tour. I am excited! Are you excited?" The tour guide's natural enthusiasm was contagious.

"Si!" everyone replied in a harmonious tone despite their differences in accents as the van took off down the street.

Being a small group, the setting was perfect for everyone to connect and exchange the stories behind their visit to Oaxaca. The narrative was very familiar to Brenée by now. People were visiting from all over the world for only one reason – to experience something new.

The tour van was soon filled by the universal sounds of random laughter and various conversations happening simultaneously.

The group embarked on their captivating journey by first visiting a unique natural wonder, Hierve El Agua, a place known for its breathtaking beauty, petrification abilities, and steam special effects. Brenée was entranced by the mesmerizing vertical cliffs dominating the distant view, petrified cascading waters frozen in time, and underground escaping gasses appearing to boil water on the surface.

"Amazing. This place is a natural paradise of illusion!" The Australian mother observed, and the tour group could not agree more.

During the tour they had a chance to wander freely and at their own pace, exploring the natural wonder of the place. Brenée found a quiet bench at one point and pulled out her mother's journal, she'd taken to keeping it on her during her travels.

Observing the scenery, she thought of her mother. *Did you write in your journals while you sat in places like this, Mom?* Opening to a place that had some white space, Brenée jotted down a few observations of Hierve El Agua. She wasn't always quite sure what was most important to document, but it felt good to sit and write, savoring the moment.

After spending three hours at Hierve El Agua, lunch time was fast approaching.

The tour guides gathered up the group and headed to a local market so they could try old-style Oaxacan cuisine. Brenée savored her taste of the region's culinary delights, such as traditional mole, tlayudas, and memelitas.

Eating at a bustling open-air market, with its loud sounds and the strong food aromas coming from all directions, was far from sophisticated dining. Yet, Brenée found there was something deeply comforting about the simplicity of the setting – almost like eating at your grandma's kitchen on an easy Sunday morning.

With a full belly and a happy heart, Brenée looked out the window as the tour van continued onward.

Next stop: the Arbol de Tule, a 2,000-year-old tree located in the courtyard of the old church of Santa Maria del Tule.

Walking with the group towards the courtyard from where the van had parked nearby, Brenée caught her first glimpses of the tree's massive canopy peeking above the surrounding buildings. It was hard for Brenée to believe that the tree was almost as old as Christianity itself.

As she turned the final corner and stepped into the tree's courtyard, the full splendor of the Arbol de Tule was revealed. Before her stood a colossal Montezuma cypress tree, also known as the Tree of Life. Brenée gently reached out and touched the trunk, in awe at the ancient life before her.

She slowly walked around the enormous trunk, which she'd learned from the tour guide had a circumference of over 36 feet.

"That's so surreal; it looks like a deer's head!" Brenée pointed out the intricate patterns and shapes coming to life on the ancient bark.

"That's right!" said Lupita, the guide. "You will find animal-like shapes all around the trunk. That's one of the reasons it's called the Tree of Life. You see the elephant over there?" she pointed to the right of the trunk.

"Ah, I do!" Brenée answered, taking a moment to snap a couple pictures of the tree. She felt, as she stood in its presence, that the Arbol de Tule was not just a tree; it was a symbol of true resilience.

It was as if over the centuries, life was documented in this living tree nestled in an enchanting corner of Oaxaca.

After a day of exploration, the tour was slowly coming to an end. The energy of the group had significantly decreased; however, even when tired, Brenée noticed that everyone in the group had a smile on their face after such a memorable experience.

Driving back through the winding roads of Oaxaca, the tour van came back to the meeting point at the artsy barrio of Jalatlaco.

"Thank you all for joining us today on this incredible journey through Oaxaca's rich history and culture," said Lupita. "It's been an honor to share these beautiful sites with you. I hope you've enjoyed exploring this amazing city and its traditions as much as we've enjoyed guiding you."

Everyone, including Brenée murmured their agreement – the tour guides had brought the city to life with their stories, knowledge, and insights.

"We hope you all have a wonderful rest of your afternoon," continued Roberto, the second guide. "And if you have any questions or need recommendations, feel free to ask us. We hope to see you back in Oaxaca soon!"

"I do have one question, actually," Brenée approached them. "I read this is an artistic area. Are there any galleries or markets I can visit on my way back to my hotel to look at local art?"

"Certainly!" Lupita replied. "Continue walking down this street for about three to four blocks until you find a church on your left. Catty-corner from there, you will see an open area with street art and boutiques. There, you will find all sorts of art – jewelry, textiles, pottery, paintings, you name it."

"Excelente!" Brenée said, following it up with a hug and kiss on the cheek as was customary in Mexico, then she set off on her own once again.

May 16th:
A Journal of Sunsets

Under a canopy of colorful papel picado banners that fluttered in the breeze, Brenée found the street market. The summer evening was still warm and bright, and Brenée heard the nearby church bell ring – announcing to the town that it was 6:00 P.M. *Plenty of time left to wander,* she thought.

Just as Lupita had said, there were handmade crafts, textiles, and whimsical alebrijes. Of course, no Mexican market is truly complete without food and live music, and there were plenty of both. Street artists at work added another layer of magic to the scene as they showcased their creative abilities.

One of the artists particularly caught Brenée's attention.

The young woman was humbly dressed with her hair tied back in a loose bun and sat cross-legged on the ground sketching some drawings with watercolors. Laid out before her was a collection of journals with colorful covers and pages made from recycled paper. The cover designs were painted by hand with immense skill and detail. No two journals were identical; each one was a unique work of art.

As she took in the artist's work, one journal captured Brenée's attention. Painted in soft hues of pink and peach was the figure of a young woman facing a sunset with the breeze sweeping her hair and blowing her dress to the side.

I love this one! Brenée thought as she reached out, feeling this might be the journal she could call her own.

"Are you the artist who paints these covers?" Brenée asked tracing the edge of the journal.

"Si, I am," replied the young woman whose eyes seemed to reflect deep passion for her art. "The title of the piece is on the back," she continued.

Brenée picked up the journal and felt a tingle of excitement as she turned it over.

A Journal of Sunsets was scrawled by hand in black ink. Something inside her clicked. *A Journal of Sunsets*, Brenée thought, *that is truly beautiful*. She smiled, now knowing this was most definitely the journal waiting for her stories.

"I'll take it," she said, clutching it to her chest as if it had already become hers.

Beneath the shade of a fully bloomed Jacaranda tree decorated with purple flowers and green foliage, Brenée found a spot to sit with her new journal. It felt as though she had discovered not only the perfect place but also the perfect moment, as the sky began its colorful transition into night.

The sun dipped lower, the light softened, and the shadows stretched, casting a serene feeling over Brenée.

With such a tranquil backdrop, Brenée took up her pen to write her opening phrase. She paused and hesitated. She had so much to write about and yet, she didn't know where to start.

Taking a deep breath, she began.

Dear Mom,

I believe today is Friday. The calendar assigns a number to the day, but in truth, the date doesn't matter, and the time is irrelevant. To me, it is only a beautiful day. Today, I've been with myself, enjoying the scenery, and walking with your presence that never leaves my side.

I've been months and miles away from dad, delivering your ashes around the world just as you wanted it and now, I feel safe. Here, I am home.

Often, I wake up at night forgetting where I'm at. There are days I miss Texas and other days where I feel I never want to go back. Here, I am home.

As much as I miss dad, I don't want to return to a life of routine; a life where every day feels on repeat with each day blurring into the next one like pages on a book with the same sentence written over and over again. Here, each day is unique with many things to experience, new things to learn, and even different challenges to figure out. I have felt uncomfortable on many occasions, but India taught me to take deep breaths and El Camino to keep placing one foot in front of the other.

Oh, and thank you for reminding me of our word, determination. It has helped me get to where I am today.

You want to know something? Back home I felt your absence deeply. Here, I feel your presence every day, all around me. I can see you in a sunset, in a mountain, and even speak to me through the breeze.

Under a colorful summer sunset in Oaxaca City, I feel you. It is as if I was meant to be nowhere else but here.

Mom, I miss you, but I know here - here, we are home.

Brenée kept writing, filling page after page. Her hands giving form to words that vastly poured out, allowing the memories to never age. Eighteen pages later, under the cover of the night, yet still sitting under the tree, she realized it was already 8:30 P.M. *Time to wrap it up and resume another day*, she thought.
She breathed deeply, savoring the warm summer night air, and penned one last thing in her journal:

P.S. Mom, you were right. There is something powerful about the written word, captured forever in time for your future self to read.

Journaling, as I'm learning, is good for the soul!

~Brenée

May 20th:
The Psychedelic Topic

After having spent four sunsets in Oaxaca City, Brenée knew it was time to move on from this colorful and charming place. She'd spent time each day with her journal, meticulously and freely pouring her memories, anecdotes, and feelings onto the pages. From the terrace to the Café to sitting under an old tree, she'd found places to get cozy and write.

Her Journal of Sunsets was now a constant companion, a friend she could confide in.

At the lobby of her Bed & Bread, Brenée found a place to sit. The space was small, yet it exquisitely captured the essence of the local indigenous cultures - rich terracotta walls created an inviting atmosphere, intricately crafted Talavera tiles featured geometric patterns with a touch of sophistication and hand-woven Zapotec rugs thoughtfully added texture to the floor.

In this inviting place, Brenée opened the pages of her mother's journal to read what instructions came next.

Hello, my Sunshine!

I hope you are enjoying Oaxaca, one of my favorite places in the world. It was difficult to decide if it was its artistry, food, or beauty that captivated my heart from the very first time. Oaxaca, as you can see, is natural, open-minded, and mystical. I call it a place of pure, organic magic.

As we keep moving forward, it's now time to leave the big city and visit a small village on the southern mountain range known for its stunning panoramic views, San José del Pacífico.

While many are drawn to the ocean, my heart always belonged to the mountains.

The mountains were my fortress, my refuge, my temple of peace. The space where the sun illuminated my mind, the air purified my thoughts, and the rocks protected me from my own fears. The mountains were the sanctuary where I would meditate, affirm, and visualize while looking at the world from a higher perspective.

San José del Pacífico isn't just surrounded by mountains- it is the mountains.

Once in this town, go to the highest top and spread the last of my ashes there. It would bring me great joy to know I, too, will be the mountains.

Happy travels,

~Mom

Without delay, Brenée started searching the web. By now, logistics felt like second nature to her, coordinating the moving parts – schedules, accommodations, and budgets.

"Going to San José del Pacífico next!" she said as she texted her dad to give an update.

Brenée boarded a shuttle to San José del Pacífico early in the morning with great excitement. After stowing her backpack in the rear, she greeted the other passengers, "Buenos dias!" taking a seat near the back.

Just thirty minutes into the ride, the van moved from urban scenery to dense forest blurring past the windows. The road began to warp around the mountainside, each curve pulling the van from side to side. Passengers swayed to the right. Then to the left. It quickly became clear the route was a sharp maze of twists and turns, winding like a loosen ribbon with each curve.

Brenée gripped the edge of her seat, her knuckles white, as she felt rolling waves in her stomach. Her vision distorted slightly as cold sweat cover her skin. She closed her eyes, but the relentless swaying only made it worse.

"Stop!" Brenée yelled and the van jerked to break on the narrow, gravel-covered shoulder. Stumbling out, she barely made it to the edge of the road before her stomach betrayed her. She leaned forward as the violent waves crashed out of her.

After a few minutes of rage, her stomach finally calmed down and Brenée wiped her mouth.

"Here, this should help you," A female voice from behind said, handing over a bottle.

"What's this?" Brenée asked, trying to focus her blurry attention on the label. "Oh, yes. Thank you. Dramamine is what I need. I had no idea the road was like this."

"Keep it if you'd like. We have plenty. This is not our first time on this wild ride," the young lady said with a smile.

"Señorita, está bien?" the driver walked towards them with concern.

"Sí, estoy mejor, I feel better," Brenée replied.

The driver kindly suggested Brenée take the front passenger seat to reduce her motion sickness and once settled, they returned to the road.

She deliberately tried to keep the view of the winding road in the horizon while taking slow, measured breaths, but something called her attention. She shifted her gaze to the dashboard uniquely decorated with bright tassels and shiny beads, bringing back memories of India. She chuckled, thinking of her mom and her invitation to find similarities between two countries worlds apart.

During her observations, she heard the same female voice behind her again.

"Where are you coming from?" she asked.

Briefly turning her head, she noticed it was the Dramamine girl, "From the Southwest of Texas," Brenée replied. "You?"

"My cousin and I come from Germany. We love it here, so we come back whenever possible. We usually start in Oaxaca City, making our way down to Zipolite. And you? Looks like this your first time in Oaxaca?" the young woman asked.

"Yes, it is. I arrived five days ago after a-month long pilgrimage in Spain walking El Camino de Santiago. Before that, I was in India for almost two months," Brenée expanded the conversation to continue distracting her mind from the road.

"Nice! I love hiking, but El Camino takes hiking to an entirely higher level. You must be a hard-core explorer!" the girl said, her eyes lighting up with excitement.

"Uhm, actually…not really," Brenée recalling her days back home, "Before traveling to India, I was pretty much a homebody," sharing a brief glimpse of her story.

"We would love to hear more about your travels, if you're up for sharing," she said. "My name is Ilse and this is my cousin Johanna," Ilse extended her arm across the rows to shake Brenée's hand. "What's your name?" she asked.

"My name is Brenée, it's really good to meet you," Brenée shook hers back. "I am staying at the Elba Cabins. What about you?"

"Everything here is within walking distance really. We are staying at the cabins next to yours, Posta de Soul," she said, trying to pronounce the Spanish words as best as she could.

"Puesta Del Sol," the driver corrected Ilse.

"That! Gracias. Si, si, my Spanish is not very good!" Ilse said with a laugh.

"We are spending only three days here. The town is super small, but it offers lots of hiking routes and plenty of opportunities to do magic mushrooms. That's what we are here for. Are you doing mushrooms too?" Johanna casually asked, joining the conversation.

"Who me? Oh, no, not at all," Brenée paused briefly. "Uhm… those are hallucinogens, right?' she asked.

"Yes, but they are more than that," Ilse replied. "In this region, people see them as sacred because of their healing powers. I mean, psychedelic mushrooms are now viewed as therapeutic. In Europe and Canada, they are used to treat mental health issues. It's amazing how many incredible benefits they've discovered! I wouldn't be surprised if more countries start to follow their lead soon."

"Yes, I've heard a bit about them," she replied feeling out of place in the conversation.

"Uhm, como se dice (how do you say) …medicine woman, healer?" Johanna asked the shuttle driver.

"Se dice curandera. Aqui hay muchas de esas," (Healer in Spanish is curandera. We have a lot of healers here), he explained.

"Yes, but this "curandera" was from the 1950s. She used to hold magic mushroom ceremonies for wealthy bankers from New York City," Johanna clarified.

"Ah, si! Maria Sabina was her name. Sadly, back then, she was considered a traitor by the town for allowing outsiders to take part in mushroom rituals. Now, it is widely accepted to open these experiences to foreigners," the driver said.

"That's right," Ilse chimed in, "actually, we have a private guide who will take us on a trail up the mountain to have a mushroom ceremony in the morning. Her name, coincidentally, is also Maria," Ilse explained. "She's a very nice and knowledgeable lady; in case you'd like to join us."

"Uhm," Brenée stalled for a moment, a whirlwind of intense emotions rolling through her at the thought of the invitation. "I've never done any psychedelics before," Brenée said. "Maybe…can I think on it? With this crazy road, I can't think clearly right now."

"Oh, of course! I completely understand," Ilse continued. "It's totally cool if you don't want to. It is a personal journey that you need to feel ready to take. Very similar to El Camino, you know?"

"Well, I was not ready to walk El Camino at all, but I did it anyway. Heck, I don't think I would have ever walked across Spain without my mom asking for it." Brenée laughed. Just out of curiosity," she continued, "So what benefits have you experienced from taking magic mushrooms? If you are comfortable sharing."

"Good luck getting her to stop talking about it, once she starts!" Johanna said with a twinkle in her eye.

"Don't exaggerate," Ilse chuckled. "But seriously, my experiences with mushrooms have been so meaningful. The biggest benefit for me has been healing my depression. I stopped taking meds a while back because I never felt like they ever helped me. I would often be drowsy or feeling just weird."

"Nature and science are not mutually exclusive, mom used to say," Brenée said with a smile. "I learned that from her!"

"Your mom was right," Johanna agreed. "As for me, I've found it's a way to connect more deeply with the universe while also having a really powerful experience that's hard to put into words."

"Thank you for sharing, and for the invitation," Brenée said. "I have to admit…I'm intrigued."

May 20th:
Running with the Bulls

Adjusting the shoulder straps of her backpack, Brenée waved goodbye to Ilse and Johanna who were still in the shuttle.

"We'll chat later, Brenée," Ilse yelled through the window as the van took off. Brenée gave her a "thumbs up" high in the air to let her know she had heard.

Walking towards the main cabin office, she took a moment to get her bearings. There was noticeable moisture in the air as the low clouds covered the sky. Colder than where she'd last come from, she felt the chill, rushing to get checked in and grab the key to her cabin.

As she pushed open the thick wooden door, Brenée was greeted by a chubby little white French bulldog lying comfortably in the warmth of the cabin.

"No te espantes. Es una perra amigable (Don't be afraid. She's a friendly dog)," the employee said, waving Brenée in. "You must be Brenée, correct?" he asked as he extended his hand.

"Hola! Yes, I am. Thank you," Brenée said in a rush.

"Bienvenida, welcome! Come on in! We are happy you are here. We were expecting you," the man continued. "This is the key to your cabin, and we will deliver wood for the fireplace around 7 P.M. We can start the fire earlier if you need us to. There are no heaters inside the rooms and as you can see, we are expecting heavy rain tonight. You will need the fire going to stay warm. If you think you will need a second load of wood, just let us know."

"Thank you, I appreciate it. I am sure I will need more wood; I am so cold. It was 89 degrees a couple of hours ago in Oaxaca City!" Brenée said.

"Welcome to the Cloud Forest! You're at high altitude now. Extra wood is no problem; not at all." he smiled. Brenée took the key and headed towards her cabin.

"Be careful and hold on to the rails when coming down," the man warned Brenée as she started descending a long inclining ramp. "The ground is slippery, and the ramps are steep," the man gave one more piece of advice.

Brenée looked up to the man nodding her head.

As she walked down, she took in the picturesque scenery. The charming cabins were located on the face of the mountain almost appearing to be hanging off the cliff. The view was simply breathtaking – tall trees, colorful vegetation, and magnificent mountain ranges that stretched before her as far as her eyes could see. The smell of fresh forest filled her nostrils, and the moist air was gentle to her skin.

"Mom, you really outdid yourself on this one," Brenée whispered in awe. "It's like an enchanted forest!" She paused on the ramp to simply soak it all in, breathing deeply.

Her tension from the curvy road loosened from her shoulders and her mind calmed as she spent those few minutes fully immersing herself in the natural richness of the Oaxacan highlands.

When she made it to her room, Brenée found it was a modest yet cozy one-bedroom cabin with walls made of stone. On the left was a small fireplace with ashes from previous fires and to the right was a tall tree growing inside the room with roots protruding from the floor. With the trunk piercing through the ceiling, the shower was strategically located underneath the indoor tree to allow the running water to nurture it. "Genius!" she said with amazement.

Brenée's now familiar routine of unpacking her backpack and making her little space feel like a temporary home was interrupted by the sound of an incoming text message.

"Hi Brenée! It's Johanna," it read, "just wanted to let you know we're meeting Maria, the medicine woman, tomorrow morning outside La Morenita Restaurant at 8:30 A.M. If you decide to join our magical experience, we'll see you there. No pressure, no stress!" As Brenée read the invitation, a familiar rush of adrenaline surged through her veins, feeling much like receiving an invite to run with the bulls in Spain.

Should I? She thought. Her thoughts swirled around the idea that this must have been the reason her mother had visited San José and considered it a place of true magic. And…perhaps, she was setting up the occasion, hoping Brenée would leap to the opportunity and say yes.

The scenery is beautiful, but people come from across the globe for one purpose and one purpose only, she thought.

Like a numinous message from her deepest depths, she heard a soft voice clearly talking to her, *Run with the bulls, Brenée.*

And with no hesitation and self-determination, Brenée replied to the voice, *"I've run with the bulls before, and I'll run with the bulls again."*

May 21st:
To Breathe Together

It was early morning in San Jose Del Pacífico when Brenée woke up after a night of non-stop rain. She lay buried beneath heavy blankets with the lingering scent of burned wood from the fireplace drifting through the air. As her eyes fluttered open, she saw the light of dawn beginning to break over the mountain range, transforming the rainy sky into a palette of vivid colors.

Surprisingly, the Sun assured her of a sunny day ahead.

In the meantime, "Brrrr, it's cold," Brenée said as her teeth chattered, and her body shivered. She managed to grab her jacket from the nearby chair and put it on as quickly as possible, without leaving her bed. With an added layer on, she rushed to start the electric kettle to make a cup of tea.

As the water heated, she did some simple standing yoga poses to warm up her body. Breathing deeply, she opened her senses to her surroundings, just like she'd learned at the ashram. She felt the air, the boiling water, and her own cold limbs warming up a bit by now.

With her tea made and her body awake, Brenée grabbed a blanket and her journal curled up in the worn rocking chair. She held her mother's journal and her own as she listened to the creaky rhythms rocking back and forth. The soft glow of the sky sparkled as she picked up her pen to write.

Starting with the date and location, she then jotted down a note that would capture the moment.

Dear mom,

Today is the day. After El Camino, this is my next pilgrimage led by the magic mushrooms in this mystical place. An inner voice tells me that this was the true reason for bringing me here. I can't quite explain it, but deep down, I feel I am right. You always used to say there are no coincidences in life; things come into your life by divine appointment, by divine time.

Well, here I am saying yes and I can hardly believe it's me agreeing to this.

I know this mission you entrusted me with won't be long enough to uncover the full length that there is. However, I am willing to dig deeper and deeper.

I am prepared and ready to go.

Love you always,

~ Brenée

At an altitude of 8,200 feet, Brenée closed her journal and leaned back into the chair, cradled in comfort. With the clouds whirling around her, she had never felt closer to the sky.

Later that day, Brenée would find out she was not only in the forest of clouds, where they enchantingly draped the trees, but had also stepped into the land of fairies hidden within the swirling breeze.

It was 7:55 A.M. when she ordered a Mototaxi (the Mexican version of a familiar Tuk-Tuk in India), taking her from the cabin to the meeting point. Brenée rode in the back, finding the commonalities of the regions as her mom said.

When Brenée arrived, she was happy to see the two girls and Maria already there.

"Buenos dias!" Maria greeted Brenée with a hug and a kiss on the cheek.

"Buenos días, Maria," Brenée replied in a soft tone. "I am Brenée. Nice to meet you! Ilse and Johanna invited me to join your group to experience this for the first time. I really don't know what to expect."

Maria looked at Brenée with gentleness in her eyes.

"Brenée, I can see you look a bit nervous, but don't be. You're about to have an unforgettable, sacred, and beautiful experience that will mark you for the rest of your life," Maria said as she delicately touched Brenée's arm. "You will be fine. Trust me. No one has ever had a bad trip...not under my care." Brenée found comfort in Maria's voice and found she fully trusted the words of the wise curandera. She smiled and nodded her head in agreement.

The four ladies got on the next available Mototaxi to take them to the head of the trail higher up the mountain. The vehicle could only fit three people in the back, but under Mexican standards, the four ladies squeezed themselves in the back of the tiny tuk-tuk with Ilse perched on Johanna's lap.

After a steep, bumpy 10-minute ride, packed in like sardines in a tin can, they arrived at the trail head and nearly tumbled out of the Mototaxi one by one. The trail was fenced by a rock wall and an iron gate that Maria opened with as much calm assurance as if it was the door of her own home.

"Por aqui (This way)," Maria invited the girls in and pointed out the path.

The ladies were greeted by an unfolding scene of natural grandeur and tranquility. After a night of rain, the mountain air was crisp and cool, carrying the faded scent of wild vegetation. The soaring peaks of the San Jose del Pacífico mountain range emerged majestically in the distance stretching endlessly into the horizon. And as they hiked higher, the landscape underwent a transformation while the trail wandered through a forest of oak, cedar and pine.

Everything was alive from the chirping of birds, the rustling of trees, to the occasional swish of small creatures.

"Maria," Brenée broke the small talk they'd been walking in. "You say you've never had anyone experience a bad trip. So bad trips don't happen?" she asked the question that had been floating in her mind.

"The sole purpose of the mushroom is to heal, Brenée," Maria promptly replied. "If you genuinely open your mind to its healing and transformative powers, the mushroom may reveal beautiful places within your psyche. However, if needed, the mushroom may also unlock places you've been purposely avoiding showing you things you may not want to see. That doesn't make it a 'bad trip,' though," she said. "The key is to learn from it and surrender to the experience. If something dark or frightening comes up, don't run away from it. Embrace it instead. And I will be there to help you if this does happen."

"That makes a lot of sense actually," Brenée said. Feeling grateful for Maria's non-judgmental explanation, Brenée felt comfortable enough to continue the conversation.

"I'm not sure how it will affect my mushroom experience, but I lost my mother last year. It's interesting how life unfolds sometimes," she said opening herself up to the experience.

"Over the past five months, I've traveled through the vibrant land of India, crossed the entire northern coast of Spain by foot, and came here without knowing why my mom chose this place," Brenée continued. "She never mentioned to me she came here to have a mushroom experience. But now, I am starting to believe my mom asked me to visit this place to experience its magic. She must've known I was going to come across it somehow. It's simply unavoidable. At least I believe that."

"I believe that too, Brenée," Ilse said, leaning in slightly.

"Perhaps, it was no coincidence we met. Maybe this is your mom conspiring to provide the ideal conditions for the perfect first time," Johanna said.

"Conspire. Do you girls know what conspire means?" the medicine woman interrupted, "It comes from the Latin roots "Con" (with) and "Spirare" (to breathe), to breathe together, to be in harmony, to be in line."

"That's fascinating – Conspire is to breathe together," Brenée had a perceptive perspective. "It makes me think about how, at its core, it's about alignment of the breath, energy, purpose. It's a reminder that yes, my mom conspired with life to create this great mission even after death."

"Well, Brenée," Maria replied. "That was a peak realization."

Easing into silent action, they continued to ascend.

As they walked, Maria prompted them to pay attention to their thoughts, their feelings, even the scenery they walked through. Her soft voice already guided them into a state of mindful awareness, preparing them for the magical journey ahead.

"Behold the view. We have arrived at our first stopping point," Maria said with a flourish towards an old wooden bench by the mountain cliff. "Wow," Brenée exclaimed joy and awe at the sight.

From this lookout point, the young woman was rewarded with a breathtaking panorama overlooking the village left behind snuggled among the foothills. Beneath them, the valley unfolded in all its glory, waking up a deeply felt sense of amazement in Brenée at the raw beauty of the big mountains.

"It is captivating, Maria! I can hardly believe the sky cleared up so nicely this morning after such rainy night. The sun is making everything sparkle…like magic," Brenée said.

"You girls are so lucky. We've been getting so much rain lately that I was prepared to guide this trip under poor conditions. But here we are – it's a lovely and bright day out indeed," Maria said, as she started taking several small packages out of her messenger bag. "These are your mushrooms," Maria announced. Wrapped in large grape leaves, the mushrooms were tucked inside, with one folded leaf given to each one.

"Open your grape leaf and you will find seven mushrooms inside. Start by taking your time to eat the first five as we enjoy the view," Maria started to give a short orientation. "Then, let your body digest them as we continue hiking up the mountain. When we get to our next stop, you will eat the other two. Remember it will take from 30 to 45 minutes for the mushrooms to take full effect depending on your metabolism. So, by the time we reach our second spot, you should be noticing the magic beginning to seep in."

Brenée paused; then, started to unwrap the grape leaf, holding each fold as a crystal snowflake, delicate and brief. She opened it to the right and then to the left exposing the small bouquet of mushrooms. The fungi blooms were small to medium in size and unlike anything she was used to, these stood out with their gray hue and slender, elongated stems. She looked at them with curiosity and attention. It was obvious they had just been picked by noticing at the bottom tip.

"Do we dust them to remove the dirt from the bottom, Maria?" she asked, eager to follow the proper protocols for the ritual.

"No, simply eat them as is. We were formed from clay, and to clay, we shall return. Make sure you eat the whole mushroom and drink water to wash them down," Maria said.

"Oh, one more thing," Maria continued. "Before you eat your first one, I recommend you ask the mushroom a question; a question that you've been waiting to know the answer for. If the time is appropriate, the mushroom may open dimensions within yourself to gift you with the answer," Maria instructed. She then guided them through several full body breaths to ground them into the moment and help them drop into a meditative state before asking their question.

In this mystical ritual, Brenée gently cradled the mushrooms in her hands as she silently asked her question. Brenée proceeded to take the first mushroom out of the bunch. To the touch, it was smooth and spongy.

Starting from the cap, she calmly took the first bite, which felt tender and soft. Picking up musky hints with rich, earthy tones, Brenée continued eating the stem, which felt fibrous to her tongue. After repeating the process four more times, she folded up her leaf again and left the remaining two mushrooms wrapped inside.

"Ready to keep going?" Maria asked. "We will continue hiking up. Be careful because it is steep and you may encounter muddy patches along the way." Maria struck out confidently, guiding them once again with her energy, her voice, and her *curandera* warmth.

The path grew continually steeper with the three girls leaning forward to climb the almost vertical trail. After 15 long minutes of climbing uphill, Johanna stopped, struggling to catch her breath.

"Can we take a moment?" she asked. "I can hardly breathe."

"The altitude must be affecting you," Maria said, reassuring that they were nearly at the next stop. After a brief rest, the medicine woman supported them to continue the climb. Ten minutes later, she gently brought them to a halt.

"Ok, we have arrived," Maria said, making a grand gesture to welcome them to a flat area just off the trail.

"It's been long enough since you ate the first five mushrooms, and the effects will soon start. Get comfortable and give each other space. We will be here for a while. You can sit or lie down on the ground. To be honest, once the effects of the mushroom start, you may move around anyway," Maria said, guiding them to eat the last two mushrooms.

Brenée, following instructions, sat down cross-legged on a bed of dry leaves and long pine needles, eventually lying down on her side with her bag under her head.

Her eyes gently stared out into the vast open blue sky when, suddenly, she focused her attention back on the ground. She could hardly believe her eyes when she saw the mountains waving and rippling, as if breathing.

She rushed to seat right back up.

The scenery around her was slowly coming alive. It was as if she was gradually stepping into another dimension where the Earth was able to expand and contract. Noticing the pine needles moving, interlacing, and weaving together, they created a rich tapestry of shapes. Brenée took a closer look and noticed how the shapes connected like textiles with golden knots.

Everything around her became vibrant, colorful, moving to the rhythm of a common dance; her senses heightened and sounds sharpened. All of nature seemed to tell a tale through the language of the forest.

Once at ease with the visual movements, Brenée lay down again. "Hhhh..." she felt the depth of the inhale, "Hhaaa..." and the length of the exhale touching the fullness of the orchestrated breath. While breathing with the Earth, she felt a profound sense of serenity and a deep connection with herself. In fact, Brenée felt as if she was conspiring with nature, breathing together with her elevated Self.

May 21st:
One with the Mountaintop

After a short thirty-minute journey, the magical movements and euphoric sensations of the mushrooms started to wear off. The feeling slowly faded, and the scenery gradually returned to normal. Looking for Ilse and Johanna, Brenée noticed they were still lying down in the distance. She turned her head in the opposite direction to look for Maria, only to find Maria already staring back at her.

"How do you feel?" Maria asked her in a soft voice.

"I feel fine. The experience revealed nature has a soul - the Earth breathing, the ground weaving, everything around me dancing in sync, but…" she paused, "I think, it's now over," Brenée said with certain discontent.

"Everyone's different. Keep in mind this was your first time," Maria said. "Come on, follow me. You see that spot up there?" Maria pointed out a place within view. "Let's climb a bit more to give you some time to reflect while giving Ilse and Johanna a few more minutes." Brenée nodded in agreement as she stood up and dusted herself off.

As they walked the short distance up the trail, they reached the point Maria had recommended. A cascading stream of crystalline waters came into view with the water tumbling over moss-covered rocks. The sound was soothing, creating a fragile melody hovering over the edge of hearing.

"We are here, Brenée," Maria pointed out. "Take a moment to enjoy. I'll come right back with the other girls."

"Thank you. This is perfect. I will wait here," The soft murmur of the trickling stream, offered a moment of relaxation amidst the rugged, steep terrain.

"By the way," Maria stopped and turned back. "Did the magic mushroom answer your question, Brenée?" she asked.

"Uhm, no. I don't think so. How would I know for sure?" Brenée asked with genuine curiosity.

"You would know, Brenée. You would know. Keep your eyes open, and in time, the answer will come to you. When it does, you will recognize it," Maria responded as she turned around and continued descending.

The answer will come to me, and I will recognize it, Brenée repeated in her mind as she sat down on a boulder next to the waters. Opening her journal she carried in her bag, she proceeded to write.

Dear mom,

Today, I witnessed nature come to life – the Earth, the Sun, the sky – organized collectively in a dance. Remember how you said all humans, to some extent, were connected in this tapestry woven by the forces of history?

Mom, after this morning, I'd stretch the thought even further and add that everything is woven by ethereal forces existing past our ordinary minds.

The concept of connection took on an entirely new significance, a more profound meaning, a deeper find. And even though the mushroom did not answer my question, I know it will come in time.

As I sit on this mountaintop, I want you to know that I did answer to all your final wishes.

Today, I complete the missions laid out in your journals with this one being the last. It's incredible to realize that even after nearly 365 sunsets without your physical body, through your writing, I still feel connected to your presence that is so alive.

Love you, mom. To the sunset and back.

~ *Brenée*

Brenée closed her journal. Sealing the moment by extending her arm over the crystal-clear waters, she sprinkled the last and final portion of her mom. Little by little, she scattered the ashes throughout the breathing forest and the smiling sky. As requested, - to the last drop - all of her mom had become one with the mountaintop.

May 21ˢᵗ:
The Shroom Therapist

Eventually Maria, Ilse, and Johanna came up to where Brenée was sitting, and shortly after that, the group began their descent back down to the trailhead.

"How long have you been bringing people up here, Maria?" Brenée asked wanting to find out more.

"I have been leading others into this kind of experiences for sixteen years now. I've helped many, each carrying their own unique journey – from curious people to mental health experts. Sometimes these professionals come by themselves; other times, they bring their clients. The mushroom is a great tool that allows patients to unlock their minds and expose what is truly behind."

"That is amazing, Maria," Johanna said. "We were just talking about that on the shuttle. I know there has been a lot of interest in the mushroom. I wouldn't be surprised if this gets officially recognized as a legit therapeutic approach by the scientific community."

"I agree," Maria said. "But it is truly surprising how much ground science still must cover in the study of the mushroom. In this region, we have been consuming mushrooms for hundreds of years. Depression and anxiety are unheard of to us. I, myself, have been doing mushrooms since I was 3 years old."

"Three years old?!" Ilse said in shock.

"Yes, three years old. My father gave me my first small amount of mushrooms at that age. I will never forget my experience. I was transported to a garden of rainbows, colors, and flowers. It was a beautiful place that I remember to this day. As said, the mushroom is sacred in this region; it is part of our culture, lives, and traditions. The mushroom is our guru, our teacher, and even our mental health therapist," Maria said, passion filling her voice.

"That is remarkable, Maria," Brenée said, then added, "My experience today felt mild and short – like skimming the surface of something vast and sacred without fully diving in. It was a beautiful moment, but it never reached that place of profound unrevealing or insight I hoped for. It was as if the door had opened just a crack offering a glimpse of what lay afar. I am ready for the door to be wide open – and this time, I want to walk through it to experience what had been spoken. Do you think it is safe for me to do it again?

"Absolutely!" Maria replied. "You can't overdose on mushrooms if you stick to the amount I give you. I can send you home with some for tonight."

"Really?" Brenée asked. "Do you think I am ready to experience this alone?"

"If you are open to it, then you are ready. The mushroom was the key that unlocked a hidden part of you and now open, it awakened a deep desire to return," Maria said.

"I do want to return!" Brenée gushed.

"We will get back into town here in a few minutes," Maria said looking at the time on her phone. "It is almost 1 P.M. I will take you all out to eat so you can have a good hearty meal. I'm sure you girls are very hungry since you haven't had breakfast. After lunch, Brenée, don't eat anything for 5-6 hours. This means that around 6 P.M. you can have your second mushroom experience. An empty stomach is necessary for the mushrooms to have a stronger effect."

"Sounds like a plan, Maria," Brenée said.

"Oh, one more thing," Maria added. "Get some food to go as well. I have a feeling you will have a very intense experience tonight and may become extremely hungry afterwards. There won't be any restaurants open by the time your trip is over, so you'll be grateful to have some food on hand. Trust me," Maria said as she handed over a grape leaf with the seven more mushrooms wrapped inside. Brenée accepted them with welcoming hands and an open heart.

"I know you are looking for answers and I hope the mushroom brings you closer to the origin of the truth. Most importantly," the wise woman paused, "to the truth of who you are, Brenée."

There is a quote that feels it was spoken by my soul, "He who trims himself to suit everyone will soon whittle himself away."

Don't let the world carve your truth from the outside in. You are here in this life to define your essence from within. Allow the mushroom to open doors to sacred spaces and you will find that truth in your being.

In a world that is always trying to make you fit the mold, Brenée, stay loyal to your soul."

May 21st:
The Tree of Golden Drips

As the sun slowly drifted across the afternoon sky, Brenée came back to her cabin and sat in the same old rocking chair. On the surface, Brenée appeared to be soothed by the gentle back and forth, but in her mind, she was lost in her imagination, re-living in great detail her time with the magic blooms.

Is it time yet? She wondered, watching the minutes slip by to her second mystical experience. The moment the clock ticked 5:45 P.M., she made up her mind - it was time.

With great anticipation, Brenée went back inside the cabin and sat on the edge of her bed. With the folded grape leaf resting on the palm of her hand, she took a moment to ask her question once again. She then carefully unfolded the leaf to pick a mushroom and gently take a bite.

The musky taste was not particularly delightful, but with every bite, she savored the moment.

Despite Maria's suggestion to pace herself, Brenée decided to have all seven all in one. Excited anticipation buzzed through her as she lay down in bed to wait for the magic effects.

About forty minutes later, Brenée's door slowly began to crack open, inviting her to step in.

Dancing lines of different colors, simulating tall, skinny, tribal figures, gradually started to appear under the indoor tree. The colors moved in slow and graceful motion, flowing from side-to-side, almost as if they were following the rhythm of a gentle slide. Her mind felt completely at ease being a spectator of this amusing display as her body felt deeply relaxed, lying cozy in bed.

With the colors dancing in a grand parade, she turned her attention to the window leading to the front porch. *Ahh!*, she gasped in delight at the sight of the tree next to the rocking chair turning gold with its branches sparkling like the precious metal. Hanging from its shining branches, the leaves were triangular in form and randomly twinkling like only diamonds could. *That is wild!* She thought as she witnessed the leaves melt into drips like liquid light in golden hush. Brenée blinked twice, amazed by the images before her eyes.

Enveloped by the surreal sight of these shimmering gateways of light and color that seemed to pulse with energy, she felt drawn deeper into the experience. Turning her attention inward, she noticed a warm sensation spreading all over her body along with a strong tingling that traced the contour of her lips. Sitting up slowly, adjusting to the visual intensity of her experience, she stretched and felt her body heat rising. To cool down a bit, she headed outside to sit in the rocking chair on the porch once more.

The temperature was slowly dropping and the air was getting crisp as the sun had disappeared below the horizon. Resting the back of her head on the rocking chair, it was too dark to distinguish any details of the vast, endless forest in front of her. However, she knew it was there, brought to life with the sounds of chirping crickets who added a relaxing melody to the panorama.

In a mood charmed by the elements, she turned her head to the cabin next door – just as the neighbors turned their lights off. Like a scene from a sci-fi movie, the light seeped out of their room before swirling around like fairies in the dark woods.

"Nature is alive again!" she realized. "Everything around me is dancing, moving and twirling with such elegance and grace!" Even in the dark, she could now perceive the life of the ferns, the trees, the critters her eyes couldn't see.

Lost in the magic of the moment, she gradually felt the vivid colors fading into darkness while the temperature had dropped even lower.

Feeling the chill and noticing her cold fingers, Brenée decided to head back inside. By then, her body felt tired, heavy and dense, taking some effort to get up from the chair. Finally standing, she went inside the room where the warmth and light immediately brought the radiant colors back into her sight.

"It is too quiet in here," she whispered as she played some music with Latin tempos to create the perfect ambiance.

Swaying gently side to side, she closed her eyes feeling the energy of the music deep within her. When her eyes fluttered open once more, the energetic grooves produced by the percussion seemed to give the rhythm a heartbeat. It felt so tangible and real, as if she could almost touch the steady pulse. A bubbling ecstasy built within her as she danced and laughed filled to the brim with pleasure, moving in harmony with the music.

That night, tucked away in a small cabin in an enchanting forest with trees of golden drips, Brenée experienced a festivity, a celebration - a sensory explosion of joy she'd never known before.

May 21st:
Stepping Into the Open Door

renée flopped down upon her bed, delight vibrating within her. As her body melted into the mattress, it became nearly impossible to distinguish the parameters of all of her body - where it started and where it ended. Along with her physical presence losing all sense of form, her ego seemed to as well dissolve. Turning into pure essence, her ego gradually transformed - Brenée was no longer Brenée; she became a tall mountain, which soon pulverized into fertile soil and, from the soil, flowers of all colors bloomed. It was an evolution, a metamorphosis, and transfiguration of energy signaling how everything in existence is in fact connected as her mom had said.

Almost like turning the page or drastically changing the radio station, Brenée moved away from transformation to art appreciation. She looked outside her window looking for the tree of golden drips and realized the precious green had turned into a checkered drawing with squares spiraling outwards from the center. Parallel to this vision, the wooden panels above the fireplace began to move in fascinating ways – undulating, shimmering, and gliding like silk with the round knots on the wood turning into the eyes of stunning peacock feathers. "Ooh!" Brenée whispered in appreciation of every bold, eclectic, and alive detail around her radiating rich imagination. For a moment, it felt as though she had stepped into a dream painted by Dalí, where reality danced with surreal beauty.

In the midst of all these artistic visions, Brenée closed her eyes, greeted by the vision of a twinkling fairy trailing a ribbon of golden dust. The fairy slowly landed by her side, and Brenée observed carefully as the fairy settled as softly as a drifting feather.

To her delight, the fairy marvelously transformed into her mom before her closed eyes.

"Brenée," her voice spoke softly. "My pretty girl, come here." the sight of her mom reached out to Brenée, pulling her tight into a hug.

"Mom!" Brenée said out loud, crying intensely as she felt the comforting presence of her mother's arms. "Mom, it's you! It's really you! I miss you so much!" Brenée cherished the love of her mom while she could.

"Don't you cry, my sunshine. You know I have never left your side. Haven't you felt I have been here with you through this journey – in every written word, in every step, and every sunset?" Brenée nodded in agreement.

"Yes, mom. I feel you here, but I don't want to go back home where I will feel the sad reality that you are no longer with me anymore!" Brenée said with great melancholy.

"Brenée, life goes on. You can't stop time or escape from it. In the human realm, you can only flow in it like an ever turning, ever expanding spiral carrying us forward into change," her mom said.

"I am learning to move to the rhythm of change, mom. It is scary at times, but I am doing my very best!" Brenée said. "I know you are, my girl," her mom countered, "Just look at you. You said yes to this experience on your own! This was you, Brenée. This was all you."

"Well, I figured this was the whole reason you wanted me to visit San José del Pacífico. Wasn't it, mom?" Brenée asked wanting to clarify her suspicions.

"They say the magic mushroom finds you when the time is right - not the other way around. I wanted you to have the opportunity to answer its call without me asking you to. And you did.

I know it was scary to say yes to the experience. I was there once. But remember, Brenée…when the unknown comes on knocking, which it often will, think of this time – don't run away from it. Open the door and face it. Many times, magic lives in the unknown.

Remember I am always by your side. I am unavoidably part of you and you of me because under the surface, as the mushroom has shown us, we share the same divine path."

With the help of the mushroom, their embraced bodies melted into one, creating a fluid stream of light that ultimately formed a spinning spiral suspended in the air.

"So, every time you need me, my girl," her mom concluded, "follow the sun from sunrise to sunset and there…I will always hold your hand."

Her voice faded away as Brenée felt her body gradually easing back into its physical form and gently reshaping itself into reality.

Opening her eyes, the brief encounter with her mother vanished; however, an intense warm feeling lingered.

"Thank you, mom. Thank you for letting me see you and feel you again in this magical moment," Brenée whispered out into the air.

In the dark of her room, Brenée slowly came back from her magical ride drifting into a deep and peaceful rest. The mushrooms had opened a door for her to enter an unknown dimension, a world, a space that led to her mom. And for that and more, she was eternally grateful.

May 22nd:
The Best Begins with Yes

Brenée woke revitalized with her senses still heightened, yet her body relaxed. She messaged her new friends, Johanna and Ilse, inviting them to breakfast so she could share her experience from the night before.

Chatting over coffee and a plate of Chilaquiles, Brenée tried her best to explain the joy she felt for having such a remarkable experience.

With heartfelt gratitude, she thanked them, realizing that without their encouragement, she would have missed the true, hidden purpose behind the journey to San José del Pacífico.

"So where are you going next, Brenée?" Ilse asked.

"Well," Brenée paused for a moment before proceeding, "I'm continuing down to Huatulco and then back to El Paso, my hometown in Texas. It's hard for me to believe my mission, which started in India months ago, is almost coming to an end. I'd never left home for more than a week when mom was alive. And yet, here I am; I have been away for months now."

"That's quite a bit of travel! Do you think it's changed you at all, being gone for so long?" Johanna asked.

"Oh definitely," Brenée said. "My view of the world is so different now that I can't see myself going back to my old life. Something inside me has drastically changed. I'm just not the same."

"Travel has expanded your perspective of life. It's kind of why we love it," Ilse said.

"So, once you're home, what will you do?" Johanna prompted.

"Once I get back, I'm going back to college to finish my degree in Finance," Brenée said. "But to be honest, I really have no interest in working at a job from 8 am to 5 pm like a slave to the clock. I realized on this trip that up until the time I left home I was thinking too small."

Brenée paused, her words slowly catching up to the swift domino of thoughts in her mind, loosened from her time with the mushrooms.

Looking into her friends' eyes, who were listening, she took a deep breath and continued.

"Mom always hoped for me to become an entrepreneur and create my own business, but you know…the idea frightened me; the thought of it would always paralyze me. I feared risks, failure, and perhaps even people's criticisms. Mom believed in my abilities to be my own boss, but I felt I didn't have what it would take to be one." She took another deep breath, realizing the magnitude of her new inner truth.

"This time away from home has shown me I move better through the world when I feel connected to the truth of who I am. I always felt like a shape that wouldn't square - forcing myself to fit a mold designed by the world!" Brenée shook her head with a smirk at the sheer absurdity.

"Then, last night, when I was doing my solo journey at the cabin, my question from earlier was answered. I've been asking for a while, what's my purpose? What lights my fire? The mushroom helped me see that I have a creative side. I felt something I haven't felt in years. It's like a feel-good certainty.

I now understand this fire inside me never really went out; it just got buried under fear. And after this magical experience, I feel it again. I feel my heart's saying, *this is it! This is who you are!* I'm not meant to fit into the world's idea of success. They've reduced success to glamour, wealth, and status, but to me, true success is to create a life that fills *me* with purpose. I'm not meant to climb someone else's ladder – I was born to build my own," Brenée said with deep passion in her voice.

"Whoa, a lot of deep stuff just landed for you, Brenée," Johanna said. "Now that you feel it, stay connected to your creative side – through journaling, traveling, breaking routines, anything really. We've all got to keep nurturing our fire because, otherwise, like you said, it will get buried again. It is easy to become slaves of routines, schedules and timesheets, chasing money and material things. There are so many people who waste their lives away doing things they hate in the name of "success". It is truly insane if you think about it. Because, really, time is the most precious asset we have, so why spend it being unhappy? Finance people talk about capital gains on investments, but what good is money when you incur purpose losses, quality of life shortfalls and fulfillment deficits?"

"I hadn't quite thought of it that way, but I like the analogy!" Brenée said.

"We had not mentioned it before," Johanna continued, "but back home, Ilse and I are business partners. We opened an after-school tutoring center four years ago. We are not rich by any stretch of imagination, but we love what we do and that keeps us going. The center offers us freedom of time, the ability to create and above all, gives us satisfaction. Sometimes we laugh, sometimes we cry when it gets tough, but at the end of the day, it feels so good to wake up and go to bed with purpose," she paused for a moment, "and that to me, Brenée, is success!"

"Nice! I didn't know that," said Brenée, looking into Johanna's eyes. "I feel like my mom shared that same knowledge with me so many times. But I guess the reality of it was that I wasn't ready to hear it, plus I didn't understand what she was trying to say anyway. It's like this trip ripped a bandage off my eyes, which was sadly preventing me from seeing clearly."

"You are young, Brenée," Ilse added. "It's okay if you didn't understand or made mistakes. That's part of growing up! The important part is that you have now valuable realizations. I didn't understand that either when I was your age. Now that I am in my 30s, I do.

Some people take years to rip off that bandage you are talking about and others," Ilse paused, "die with it on!"

"I can say traveling helps get those realizations faster. You are exposed to different realities and get to meet people who think different than you…traveling simply opens your mind," Ilse said.

"Maybe travel can be part of your creativity, like Maria talked about," Johana suggested. "You could pick a place every year that you've never been to before and make it a point to go, explore and learn from other cultures. Maybe you can volunteer at a place where they can provide a room for you to stay, like you did in India. That can alleviate some expenses. Don't let money be the stopping factor. There are many ways of making it happen."

"Yes! I had thought about it already. This mission mom sent me on woke up something beautiful in me, and I can't let it go back to sleep anymore," Brenée said.

"That's amazing, Brenée. This is the best time of your life to explore," Johanna said. "And speaking of exploring, why don't you continue your last leg of the journey with us? We are going south to Zipolite next, which is only an hour away from Huatulco, your final destination."

"Oh, yes! I'd love to join you on one last adventure before heading home," Brenée said. "So, what is good there?"

"Zipolite is a nice small town with good vibes, hippie feels, and nude beaches," Ilse said in a casual tone.

"Nude beaches in Mexico?" Brenée asked with a laugh.

"Oh yeah! Right here in Oaxaca," Johanna said. "It's a bit wild if you think about how traditional and religious the Mexican culture is. But that is exactly the reason why we come back to Oaxaca over and over again. The mindset is very open here. And know that nudity is completely optional in case you don't feel comfortable," Johanna added.

Sipping on her coffee, Brenée felt her heart thrill at the idea. "Well, I have never done anything like that, but I am willing to follow the path wherever it lands!" Brenée said, embracing the woman her mom saw in her, the woman who knew the best begins with Yes!

May 23rd:
Nude Body, Nude Soul

The next morning, the three ladies took the shuttle to Zipolite, leaving right at 9 A.M. Predicting the road down south was going to be equally as winding as coming up to San José, Brenée prepared herself by taking her meds.

After being on a zigzagging road for three hours, they arrived in Zipolite where the hippie vibes Ilse had mentioned were instantly visible – a shirtless guy with long dreadlocks exercising under the sun, others walking barefoot on the road, and a group of girls carrying yoga mats either coming or going to class. The town seemed to move slowly, as if the word stress barely existed here.

The shuttle arrived at the bus terminal and Brenée and the German duo walked the short distance to their rental place.

"Everything here is within walking distance. It's hard to get lost," Ilse shared as she unlocked the front door. Johanna led the way into the chic white condo with navy blue accents throughout the room. At the center of the living room sat a coffee table with a decorative black sea anchor that was perfectly in line with the big glass sliding doors facing the ocean.

"Oh my gosh! Look at this amazing view!" Brenée said in excitement as she opened the curtains to reveal the entire sight.

"Right?! We always choose this place for that same reason," Johanna said.

"Well, yeah! No doubt," Brenée replied with a bit of playful sass as she vigorously opened one of the big sliding doors to step out onto the sand.

"Not so fast, Brenée," Ilse stopped her. "There is plenty of time to enjoy the beach this afternoon! Let's go eat lunch first. We know a very good Thai restaurant that we are sure you will love," Ilse said.

"That sounds wonderful! I'm excited to go along with your ideas for the stay," Brenée said with a smile.

"Let's go!" And leaving their bags unpacked, the three young ladies headed out into town.

The Thai restaurant was an outdoor place where they sat by the ocean under a tall banana tree. After enjoying a feast of shareable meals and colorful cocktails, they strolled down the main street to window shop and checked out the different outdoor activities they could enjoy over the next few days.

By the time evening rolled around, they started heading out toward the ocean to a spot called Playa del Amor (Love Beach), which they told Brenée was a less crowded place to sit and savor the sunset.

Upon arrival, Brenée instantly noticed how secluded the place felt with giant sea stacks naturally providing some privacy right on the shore. The sun was beginning its descent on the horizon, casting a warm, golden hue across the sandy beach. The breeze carried the scent of saltwater and naturally cooled her down from the afternoon's heat.

The rhythmic sound of the waves gently lapping at the shore created a soothing backdrop to the dreamy scene.

Brenée took in her surroundings, noticing a guy with a serene smile sunbathing naked on the sand playing a ukulele with its melodic tones filling the air.

The tunes of island roots danced on the breeze, connecting with the murmurs of the ocean.

As he played, he stared out at the sun and sang a heartfelt song like a love song to the ocean. The lighthearted lyrics expressed his genuine happiness and gratefulness, lifting up Brenée's spirits with his optimistic energy.

Allowing herself to sink fully into the present moment, the sound of the ukulele and the chill lyrics became an intimate bubble for Brenée. The rest of the world fell away including her friends, and only the sun, the music, and the ocean remained.

As the sun dipped lower, creating sparkles floating on the water, Brenée started removing her clothes. Letting the rhythm of the evening guide her movements, Brenée soon found herself nude in the outdoors.

A feeling of self-consciousness never crossed her mind. Instead, she felt completely comfortable in her own skin. With a sense of freedom as deep and boundless as the ocean before her, her bare feet and bare soul began dancing there - where the land ended and the sea crossed.

She opened her arms wide towards the soft, orange glow of the setting sun. The waves encouraged this beautiful moment, and Brenée thanked her mom with a quiet prayer of love.

Mom, she thought, *Thank you for the perfection of this moment of joy. Thank you for guiding me, for helping me discover my voice.*

The sunset guided the sun in the distance behind the water, trailing robes of rose and gold melting into each other until gradually blending into darkness. This marked the last breath of the day – and the first of a new chapter.

After 108 days of sunsets, she no longer felt small. Once a quiet girl of rounded posture and timid voice, Brenée was now a young woman clothed in confidence, nude and tall.

May 24th:
The Trip to the Core

After saying goodbyes to Ilse and Johanna back in Zipolite, Brenée found herself settling into her airplane seat once again just as she had done plenty of times before. This time though, it was different - it was the flight back to her Texan home.

With only six hours and forty-nine minutes to go, Brenée was to end her mother's journey, a journey defined by the numerous sunsets she had witnessed.

"On the plane. On my way home!" Brenée posted a picture of herself with a big smile to update her social media account, which she had forgotten about. Then, she texted her dad to let him know the details of her arrival.

Instantly, comments started coming in on her phone.

"Safe travels, beautiful!"

"Let's plan something soon!"

"Miss you already, Brenée!"

It was incredible to see the overwhelming number of new friends she'd met from around the world, and the countless miles she traveled around the globe.

Brenée felt a sense of accomplishment unlike any she'd experienced before. She'd done it. She'd spread her mother's ashes around the world, just like Elena had wanted.

She'd grieved, she'd grown, and stepped into a new sense of self.

Brenée reached for her journal, as it was now her common practice, to capture memorable times. Pulling her journal and her mom's out of her bag, a folded piece of paper fell out of the pages and onto the floor. *A note?* she thought as she reached for it, appearing her mom had tucked in a few more lingering words.

With great anticipation, Brenée opened it up and proceeded to read her mother's final written words:

Hello, my Sunshine,

You made it all the way through these last lines.

First and foremost, know that I am so very proud of your sense of adventure, tenacity, and stubbornness to accomplish my wishes from beginning to end. You are a remarkable and beautiful woman with a strong force that will carry you through any challenge life may throw your way.

Today, as you read this last message, I need to confess the truth; the real reason behind my final wishes.

This journey was never about me, my ashes, or my death wishes. All along, this journey was about you and the journey to your soul.

My role as your mom was not to make your life effortless; it was to make you capable. I wanted to give you everything you need to navigate the life that lies beyond the sunset and the profound travels within.

You went to India not only to learn about their heritage and culture, but to be around those in need due to the complex social issues humanity faces. Living in a country of abundance such as the one we live in, it is easy to forget the current state of the world.

India helped you explore the unfamiliar, shifted your perspective, and exposed you to disciplines outside your comfort zone. India not only expanded your mind – it also made it flexible.

You visited Spain to physically challenge your body by walking the entire northern coast through sunshine and rain.

At first, I'm sure you were doubtful, but eventually, you became good at reaching inside and finding determination - the kind that fueled your strength and kept expanding for as long as you continued walking. You didn't just arrive - you claimed the journey through effort, grit, and strength of mind.

Also, on El Camino, you found out you were not alone. On the path, you met your tribe. You came across pilgrims with whom you connected and for days, they were part of your story, and you were part of theirs. This perfectly illustrates how everything in life is intertwined.

El Camino fueled your determination and showed that your body will always adapt and respond.

And lastly, you went to Oaxaca, the door to magical experiences, the portal to your origins, the sanctuary of your soul.

Oaxaca is a place of immense creativity where I know that you were invited to come face-to-face with your essence. Here, your superficial ego melted and something of great substance was revealed to you – your soul.

Oaxaca showed you the truth – the truth of who you are – and it will now endure until the end of time. Remember to nurture your soul, care for it, and protect it. Create something beautiful, make space for stillness, and learn when to dance the song before the night is gone. The soul is fed with meaningful, creative, and mindful experiences, not just accomplishments.

Your trip to India, Spain, and Oaxaca represent your mind, body, and soul – the three sacred elements needed for the trip to your core.

Let this sequence be a reminder that you are also like a single thread in an endless quilt of existence, connected to every other piece. Just as your mind, body, and soul unite to form your being, in the same manner, you are shaping and being shaped by the infinite patterns of the world.

Life surrounds you in intricate layers – miniscule worlds thriving beneath your feet and giant worlds alive beyond your gaze. Embrace your place in this boundless, interconnected life, for you are both a part of its grandeur and a reflection of its wonder.

I am now gone from the physical place and won't be here to protect you like I did when you were small. My guidance, however, will always be with you and, for as long as you keep your hand open, I will hold yours.

I am here to help you sail through the rough waves of life. Beyond human separation, always remember that my love transcends space and time. When you need me, I am not to be found in a grave. I am now everywhere and anywhere - at the top of the mountain, in the glow of a sunset, in the crash of a wave.

Brenée, my Sunshine, whatever comes next will not be easy because what comes next is the rest of your life. I lean on the knowledge that you have now acquired the tools to walk a journey with life's hills and valleys.

No matter how wild the path gets with unexpected twists and turns, I will always be there firmly as your standing stone.

And after the sun sets and darkness takes hold, find your own destiny not in the stars, but in the light within shining as bright as gold.

This, my girl, concludes your travel inward crafted for transformation – where every step led you to explore the deepest corners of your soul.

Always remember that life is not about the journey you travel to; it's about the journey unfolding within.

Love you to the sunset and back,

~Mom

-------- **THE END** --------

A Journey

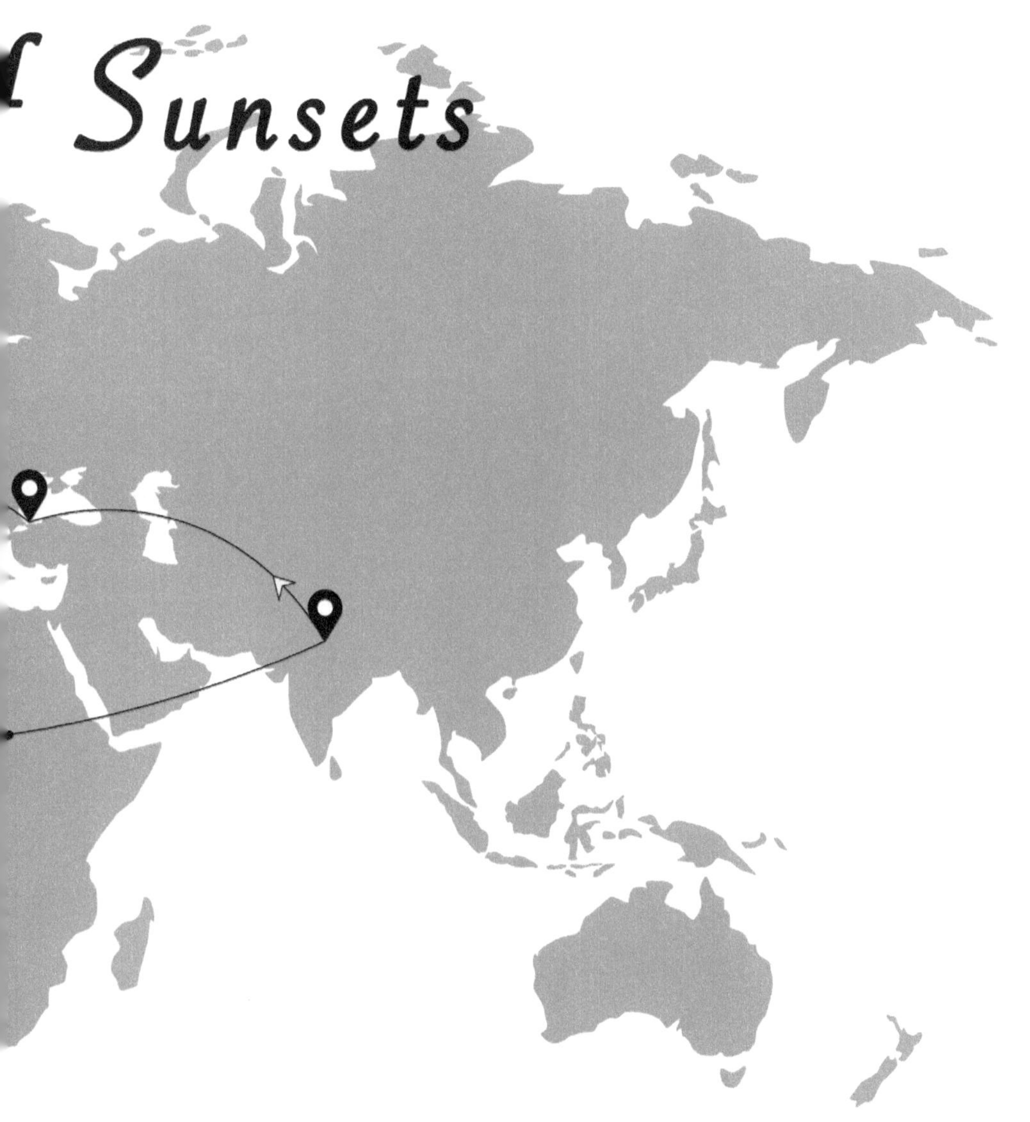
Sunsets

Reflections on A Journey of Sunsets

Reflections on A Journey of Sunsets

Reflections on A Journey of Sunsets

Reflections on A Journey of Sunsets

Reflections on A Journey of Sunsets

Disclaimer:
A Note on Reality and Fiction:

The events and characters in this book are inspired by real-world events, locations, and historical figures. However, this is fundamentally a fictionalized account. The purpose of this story is not to serve as a history lesson, but to offer a dramatic exploration of a specific time and place in the author's imagination.

Any resemblance to persons, living or dead, is largely coincidental or is used under the umbrella of historical fiction to enhance the narrative.

About the Author

A Portrait in a Few Words
In the desert landscape of El Paso, Texas, a border city where the United States meets Mexico, my childhood unfolded in a world shaped by two languages, two cultures, and the dynamic space where they intertwine. Growing up alongside my brother, who faced severe mental and physical challenges, profoundly

shaped my perspective on life. Witnessing his resilience, my mom's unstoppable courage, and mamabuela's (grandma's) faithful love taught me to recognize beauty and possibility where others might have overlooked it. This life experience eventually guided me to be of service to my community by becoming a yoga instructor and opening AeroZen Yoga Studio.

I am a mom to Benjamin Liam and Nadia Renée (both make up Brenée), who inspired me to write this book - an attempt to put into words my love for them, which expands with every breath I take. I am also a life partner to Alex with whom I now travel side by side to seek out the extraordinary in the ordinary.

One of my greatest pleasures is the search for memorable coffee shops around the globe, savoring both unique flavors and the stories captured in a good cup of coffee. I also delight in journaling, preserving with words the thoughts, emotions, and important experiences that define my life.

The sunset often finds me running at McKelligon Canyon, located in the Northeast of El Paso, where the mountains become both my endless source of inspiration and the sanctuary of my soul.